Belkin's Stories

AND

A History of
Goryúkhino Village

Alexander Pushkin

Translated by Roger Clarke

Series editor: Roger Clarke

ALMA CLASSICS

ALMA CLASSICS
an imprint of

ALMA BOOKS LTD
Thornton House
Thornton Road
Wimbledon Village
London SW19 4NG
United Kingdom
www.almaclassics.com

Belkin's Stories first published in Russian in 1831
A History of Goryúkhino Village first published in Russian in 1837
This translation first published by Alma Classics in 201
A new edition first published by Alma Classics in 2019
This new edition first published by Alma Classics in 2021

Translation, Introduction, Notes and Extra Material © Roger Clarke, 201

Cover: Nathan Burton Design

Printed in Great Britain by CPI Group (UK) Ltd, Croydon, CR0 4YY

MIX
Paper from
responsible sources
FSC
www.fsc.org   FSC® C013604

ISBN: 978-1-84749-351-4

Contents

Alexander Pushkin (1799–1837)

Abram Petrovich Gannibal,
Pushkin's great-grandfather

Sergei Lvovich Pushkin,
Pushkin's father

Nadezhda Osipovna Pushkina,
Pushkin's mother

Natalya Nikolayevna Pushkina,
Pushkin's wife

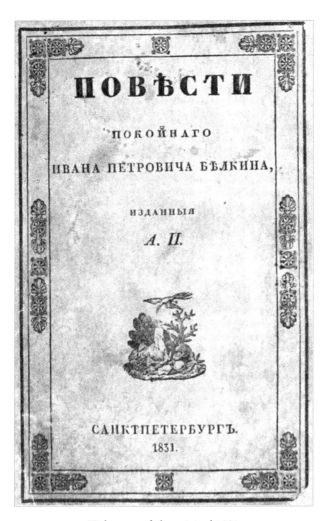

ПОВѢСТИ

покойнаго

ИВАНА ПЕТРОВИЧА БѢЛКИНА,

изданныя

А. П.

САНКТПЕТЕРБУРГЪ.
1831.

Title page of the original 1831
edition of *Belkin's Stories*

Illustration for 'The Undertaker'
by M.E. Malyshev (1887)

Publisher's Foreword

This is one of a series of volumes being published by Alma Classics that will present the complete works of Alexander Pushkin in English. The series will be a successor to the fifteen-volume *Complete Works of Alexander Pushkin* published by Milner and Company between 1999 and 2003, the rights to which now rest with Alma Classics. Some of the translations contained in the new volumes are reprints or revisions of those in the Milner edition, others are entirely new – as with this edition of *Belkin's Stories* and *A History of Goryúkhino Village*, which replaces Volume 8 of the Milner set. The aim of the series is to build on the Milner edition's work in giving readers in the English-speaking world access to the entire corpus of Pushkin's writings in readable modern versions that are faithful to Pushkin's meaning and spirit.

The Milner edition volumes were only available in hardback and as a set. Alma Classics, however, are offering the present Pushkin in English paperbacks for purchase individually.

In publishing this series Alma Classics wish to pay a warm tribute to the initiative and drive of the late Iain Sproat, managing director and owner of Milner and Company and chairman of the original project's editorial board, in achieving the publication of Pushkin's complete works in English for the first time. Scholars, lovers of Pushkin and general readers wishing to gain knowledge of one of Europe's finest writers owe him the heartiest admiration and gratitude.

– Alessandro Gallenzi

Introduction

This book contains two prose works by Alexander Pushkin, both written in the autumn of 1830: his *Belkin's Stories*, which was published in 1831, and his *History of Goryúkhino Village*, which he never published and left uncompleted when he died in 1837. *Belkin's Stories* was Pushkin's first completed and published work of prose fiction.

Belkin's Stories (*Póvesti Bélkina* in Russian) has usually gone under the English title of *The Tales of Belkin*. I have changed the English title for two reasons. First, there is ambiguity in *The Tales of Belkin*: it could be understood either as "The Tales *about* Belkin" (wrongly) or as "The Tales *produced by* Belkin" (correctly); "Belkin's Stories" makes this clearer. Secondly, the word "tales" is misleading, because it is used in English of stories about long ago or stories that are fanciful and improbable; but Belkin's stories are set within the historical Russia of Belkin's (and Pushkin's) lifetime, and Belkin claims that they are "in large part true". "Tales" is therefore a misnomer.

The presentation of *Belkin's Stories* is unusual and complex. The work purports to be a set of five stories that Iván Petróvich Belkin has heard from four different narrators and written down; the stories are prefaced by a short foreword entitled "From the

Editor", a man identified in the first edition simply as "A.P.", who has allegedly come into possession of the now deceased Belkin's manuscript and is publishing the stories along with biographical data about Belkin that he has obtained from a friend of the dead man. But this framework, too, is fictional: Belkin is as much a creation of Pushkin as the five stories, and for this reason the foreword itself is sometimes described as a sixth story.

On the surface Belkin's five stories are straightforward: clear, fast-moving, easy to read. The plots hold the attention right up to the (usually surprising) denouement; the characters are well drawn, true to life and intriguingly open-ended; there is plenty of humour; and (save in the mock formality of the foreword) the writing is lucid and terse – "precision and brevity" were Pushkin's watchwords for prose writing. But the smooth surface of the *Stories* is deceptive. Underneath, as explained in the Extra Material (p. 165), there are strong currents and cross-currents that can carry the reader in unexpected directions. One particularly powerful current is that of literary parody and allusion. Pushkin is constantly calling up other literary works, then mimicking them, subverting them or using them to deepen our understanding of plot and character. Another current is that of autobiography: Pushkin frequently smuggles events and situations from his own life into the *Stories*. Still deeper down, notably in the foreword, political currents can be discerned, carefully hidden though they had to be from the imperial censorship.

A History of Goryúkhino Village is a separate work, but linked to the *Stories* because it too purports to have been written by Belkin. Much of it is taken up by a discursive autobiography of the author, filling out the information supplied in the foreword to the *Stories*. The *History* is a comic work, making fun of certain current historians and other writers and their intellectual and literary pretensions and venturing a guarded critique of conditions in the Russian countryside. Both the parody and the social comment are more overt than in the *Stories*, which is no doubt why, before Pushkin had completed the work, he realized that the censors would never pass it for publication.

Readers will get much enjoyment from a simple read of both these works of Pushkin's, but those with the time and interest are recommended to explore the main subtexts through the Notes and the Extra Material in this volume. This will heighten their appreciation of two entertaining and intriguing pieces of Russian literature and of their author.

– Roger Clarke
April 2014

The Late Iván Petróvich Belkin's Stories

EDITED AND PUBLISHED BY A.P.

> MRS PROSTAKÓVA: You see, my dear sir, he's
> loved his stories ever since he was little.
> SKOTÍNIN: Mitrofán takes after me.
> – *The Young Hopeful**

From the Editor

When we undertook the task of publishing I.P. Belkin's stories, which we are now presenting to the public, we wanted to preface them with a résumé, however brief, of the late author's life; our wish was thereby to satisfy in some measure the legitimate curiosity of those who love our Russian literature. We intended to turn for this purpose to Márya Alexándrovna Trafílina, Iván Petróvich Belkin's heiress and next of kin; but sadly she was unable to provide us with any information about the deceased, as she had been entirely unacquainted with him. She advised us to make application to a respected gentleman who had been Iván Petróvich's friend. We took this advice and received the following welcome response to our letter. Let us print it, without any alteration or comment,* as the precious memorial of a lofty mind and of a touching friendship – and as a fully adequate biographical record.

My Dear Sir, —— ——,
I had the honour to receive on 23rd of this month your most esteemed letter of 15th of the same, in which you inform me of your wish to learn particulars of the dates of birth and death, the career, the domestic circumstances and also the pursuits and

qualities of the late Iván Petróvich Belkin, once my true friend and neighbouring landowner. It is with great pleasure that I give effect to your wish and forward to you, my dear Sir, all that I can recollect both from his discourse and from my own personal observation.

Iván Petróvich Belkin was born in 1798 of honourable and noble parentage in the village of Goryúkhino. His late father, Captain Pyótr Ivánovich Belkin, had married Pelagéya Gavrílovna, of the Trafílin family. He was not a wealthy man, but abstemious and, in the field of estate management, extremely capable. Their son received a basic education from the local parish clerk. It was evidently to this esteemed personage that he owed his enthusiasm for reading and for endeavours in the field of Russian letters. In 1815 he enlisted with a light infantry regiment (which of them I do not recall), in which he continued to serve right up to 1823. The deaths of his parents, which occurred almost at the same time, obliged him to apply for a discharge and travel back to Goryúkhino, his ancestral property.

Once in control of the estate, Iván Petróvich, by reason of his inexperience and pliancy, neglected its management and relaxed the strict regime that his late father had established. He dismissed the punctilious and alert village elder, with whom his peasants (in their usual way) were discontented, and he entrusted the administration of the village to his aged house-keeper, who had gained his confidence by her skill at storytelling.

4

This foolish old woman was never able to distinguish a twenty-five rouble note from a fifty; the peasants, who all saw her as their auntie, had no fear of her whatsoever; the village elder whom they elected indulged and abetted their trickery to the point where Iván Petróvich was forced to abolish their compulsory farm labour and introduce a very modest rent in lieu. Even then the peasants exploited his weakness and won themselves a special waiver for the first year; then in subsequent years they paid two thirds and more of the rent in cobnuts, cranberries and suchlike – and there were still arrears.

As an erstwhile friend of Iván Petróvich's late father, I considered it a duty to proffer my advice to the son too, and I repeatedly volunteered to re-establish the old regime that he had allowed to lapse. For this purpose I rode to his place one day, demanded the estate ledgers, summoned the rascally elder and engaged in an examination of the records in Iván Petróvich's presence. At first the young squire took to following me with all possible diligence and attention. It transpired, however, from the accounts that over the past two years the number of peasants had risen while the number of poultry and cattle were said to have fallen. At that point Iván Petróvich, satisfied with this initial information, listened to me no further; and at the very moment when my investigations and strict questioning had brought the rogue of an elder to total confusion and had reduced him to absolute silence, I heard Iván Petróvich, to my intense annoyance, snoring loudly in his chair. From that time on I ceased to interfere in his domestic dispensations and delivered up his affairs (as he did himself) to the dispensation of the Almighty.

Nevertheless, this did not in the least disturb our friendly relations; for I felt sorry for Iván Petróvich's feeble-mindedness and the ruinous indolence that is so common in young noblemen of our day, and I was genuinely fond of him. Indeed one could not help liking such a gentle and honest young man. For his part, Iván Petróvich always showed respect for my age and was deeply attached to me. To the very end of his life he met me almost every day, valuing my straightforward manner of talk, even though for the most part we resembled each other neither in way of life, nor in turn of mind, nor in character.

Iván Petróvich led a most abstemious life and shunned any kind of excess; I never observed him "under the influence" (which in our parts can be counted an unprecedented phenomenon). It is true that he had a marked susceptibility to the female sex, but there was in him a quite virginal shyness...[1]

Besides the stories that you are pleased to mention in your letter, Iván Petróvich left a multitude of manuscripts, some of which have found their way into my possession, though others have been used by his housekeeper for various domestic requirements. Thus last winter all the windows of her quarters

---

1 There follows an anecdote that we have not included here, deeming it superfluous; let us assure the reader, nevertheless, that it contains nothing prejudicial to Iván Petróvich's memory.

were stuffed up with the first section of a novel that he had left unfinished. The aforementioned stories were apparently his first venture. According to Iván Petróvich, they are in large part true and had been picked up by him from various individuals.[1] *Nonetheless, almost all the personal names in them he invented himself; and the appellations of estates and villages he borrowed from our neighbourhood, which accounts for my own estate being mentioned somewhere;* this occurred not from any ulterior motive, but simply from lack of imagination.*

In the autumn of 1828 Iván Petróvich came down with a feverish cold, which developed into influenza, and he died, notwithstanding the untiring efforts of our local doctor, a man of the greatest skill, especially in the treatment of chronic complaints like corns and so on. He passed away in my arms in his thirtieth year and was buried in Goryúkhino village church, close to his late parents.

Iván Petróvich was of middling height; he had grey eyes, fair hair, a straight nose and a pale and gaunt complexion.

There you have, my dear Sir, all that I can recall pertaining to the way of life, activities, character and outward appearance of my late neighbour and friend. But in the event that you think fit to use this letter of mine in any way, I most humbly ask that

---

1   In fact, in Mr Belkin's manuscript there is written in the author's hand above each story: "Heard by me from [such-and-such a person]" (with rank or position, and initials). We record for interested researchers: 'The Postmaster' was narrated to him by Titular Counsellor A.G.N.; 'The Shot' by Lieutenant Colonel I.L.P.; 'The Undertaker' by the manager B.V.; and 'The Blizzard' and 'Young Miss Peasant' by Miss K.I.T.

you make no mention whatsoever of my name; for, although I have the greatest respect and liking for writers, I see no point in entering that profession; and indeed, at my age, it would be unseemly.

With the most sincere regards, etc.

Nenarádovo village, 16th November 1830*

We consider it our duty to respect the wish of our author's esteemed friend, so let us offer him our deepest thanks for the information furnished to us, and hope that the public will appreciate the honesty and good nature with which it has been provided.

– A. P.*

The Shot*

We fought a duel.
                    – Baratýnsky*

I swore to shoot him dead, as
duelling rules allowed. (It was
now my turn to shoot.)
– 'An Evening under Canvas'*

WE WERE STATIONED in a little place called ——. A regular officer's routine is well known: mornings, drill and horsemanship; dinner with the regiment's colonel or in a Jewish tavern; evenings, punch and cards. In —— there was not a single house offering hospitality, and not a single marriageable girl. We used to congregate in each other's quarters, where all we saw were our own uniforms.

There was just one chap in our circle who was not a soldier. He was about thirty-five – so to us an old man. Experience set him above us on many counts, and a habitual surliness, an abrupt manner and a malicious tongue gave him a strong hold on our youthful minds. A certain mystery clung round his life: he seemed Russian, but had a foreign name. He had once served in the hussars, successfully too. No one knew what had impelled him to resign his commission and settle in that wretched little place, where he lived at once both frugally and extravagantly: he forever went round on foot in a threadbare black coat, but he would keep open house for all the officers of our regiment. True, his dinner consisted of just two or three courses, cooked by an ex-serviceman, but for all that the champagne flowed like a river. No one knew either his wealth or his income, and no one dared question him on it. He had plenty of books, mostly about warfare, but novels too. He would readily lend them out to read, never demanding them back; conversely, a book he had borrowed he never returned. His main pastime was pistol shooting. The walls of his room were all riddled with bullet holes, all crazed like a honeycomb. A huge collection of pistols was the only luxury in the clay-walled cottage where he lived. The skill he had attained was amazing, and if he had proposed shooting a pear off anyone's cap, no one in our regiment would have baulked at offering him his head. Our conversation frequently touched on duels; but Silvio (that is what I shall call him) never took part. If we asked if he had ever fought a duel, he would answer tartly that he had, but never went into detail; and it was clear that he found such questions distasteful. We supposed that a hapless victim of this grim sport was weighing on his conscience. Certainly it never entered our heads to suspect him of anything like cowardice. There are people whose very bearing banishes such suspicions. An unexpected incident surprised us all.

One day some ten of us officers were dining at Silvio's. We were drinking in our usual way – that is, very heavily. After the meal we began to urge our host to open us a bank for cards. For long he resisted, as he hardly ever played. But eventually he sent for cards, spread fifty ten-rouble coins on the table, and sat down to deal. We clustered round him, and the game commenced. It was Silvio's practice at cards to keep absolute silence. He never argued, and never offered explanations. If a punter miscalculated, Silvio immediately either paid up the shortfall or noted down the excess. We were aware of this, and never tried to stop him hosting the game his own way. But among us was an officer who had been newly transferred. He joined in the game at once, and inadvertently doubled the stake. Silvio took some chalk and entered the higher figure in his usual way. The officer, believing that the mistake was Silvio's, launched into protests. Silvio continued to deal in silence. The officer, losing patience, took a duster and rubbed out what he took for an incorrect entry. Silvio took the chalk and made the entry again. The officer, inflamed by the wine, the game and the company's laughter, felt himself cruelly wronged; in his fury he seized a bronze candlestick off the table and launched it at Silvio, who barely managed to dodge the blow. We were aghast. Silvio stood up, turned pale with wrath and, eyes flashing, said: "My good sir, be so kind as to leave, and give thanks to God that this took place in my house."

We were in no doubt what would follow and considered our new comrade a dead man already. The officer went out, having declared that he was ready to answer for the offence in whatever way Mr Banker pleased. The game continued a few minutes longer; but we sensed that our host was in no mood for playing, so we gave up one after another and dispersed to our rooms, chatting about the forthcoming vacancy.

The next day at horse-riding we were already asking if the wretched lieutenant was still alive, when he turned up among us in person. We all put the same question to him. He replied that he had no news yet about Silvio. That surprised us. We walked to Silvio's and found him outdoors, lodging bullet after bullet into an ace that had been stuck to the gate. He received us in his usual fashion, saying not a word about the previous day's incident. Three days passed; the lieutenant remained alive. Surprised, we kept wondering if Silvio was really not going to fight. Silvio did not fight. He accepted the briefest of apologies and made his peace.

This might well have done him huge damage in the eyes of us youngsters. A failure of courage is the most unpardonable thing of all to young people, who normally see daring as the peak of all human virtues and as an excuse for every vice imaginable. Nonetheless, it was all gradually forgotten, and Silvio regained his earlier ascendancy.

I alone could no longer warm to him. By nature I had a romantic imagination, and till now I had felt a stronger bond than anyone with a man whose life was an enigma and whom I had viewed as the hero of some mysterious tale. He was fond of me; at least, I was the only one with whom he put aside his normal cutting and ill-humoured way of speaking and talked of various matters straightforwardly and with uncharacteristic civility. But after that unhappy evening the thought that a stain on his honour had been left unexpunged at his own choice… that thought never left me and stopped me behaving to him as I had before. I felt ashamed to look at him. Silvio was too alert and experienced not to see this and divine its cause. It seemed to rankle; at least I noticed in him once or twice a wish to have it out; but I avoided such openings, and Silvio gave up on me. From then on I only met him in the company of friends, and our old frank conversations came to an end.

Harassed St Petersburgers have no concept of many sensations that are so familiar to those who dwell in the country or in small towns – looking forward to the day the mail is delivered, for example. On Tuesdays and Fridays our regimental headquarters was filled with officers, some expecting money, some letters, some newspapers. Packets were usually unsealed on the spot, news was exchanged, and the office presented a scene of the utmost animation. Silvio too used to receive letters through our regiment and was usually there. On one occasion he was delivered a packet from which he tore the seal with an expression of extreme impatience. As he scanned the letter his eyes flashed. The officers were each preoccupied with their own mail and noticed nothing.

"Gentlemen," Silvio addressed them, "circumstances demand my immediate departure. I shall travel tonight. I hope you won't refuse to dine with me for the last time. I expect *you* too," he continued, turning to me, "I expect you, without fail." With these words he left in haste. The rest of us agreed to meet at Silvio's and went off each to our own place.

I arrived at Silvio's at the time arranged and found almost the whole regiment there. All his belongings were already packed. Nothing was left but the bare bullet-riddled walls. We sat down at table. The host was in excellent humour, and his good spirits soon spread through the company. Corks popped by the minute; glasses frothed and hissed without interruption; and in the heartiest manner possible we wished the traveller a safe journey and every good fortune. It was already late in the evening when we got up from table. As we sorted our caps, Silvio bade everyone goodbye, but just as I was preparing to leave he took me by the arm and said softly: "I need to speak with you." I stayed behind.

The guests had departed; the two of us remained. We sat opposite each other and lit our pipes in silence. Silvio was sunk in thought; there was no longer any trace of his compulsive cheerfulness. His sombre pallor, his gleaming eyes and the thick smoke that issued from his mouth gave him the look of a devil incarnate. A few minutes passed before Silvio broke the silence. "It may be that we shall never meet again," he said. "Before we part I wanted to explain myself to you. You may have noticed that I've little respect for the opinions of strangers; but you I'm fond of, and I sense that it would weigh heavily on me to leave a false impression in your mind."

He paused and began to fill his pipe, which had burnt out. I lowered my eyes and kept silent.

"You thought it strange," he continued, "that I didn't demand satisfaction from that drunken idiot R—. You'll acknowledge that, entitled as I was to choose the weapon, I had his life in my hands, while my own was all but out of danger. I could attribute my restraint to pure magnanimity, but I don't want to lie. If I could have punished R— without endangering my life at all, then I'd not have let him off for anything."

I looked at Silvio in astonishment. Such an admission completely baffled me. Silvio continued:

"That's it precisely. I've no right to expose myself to death. Six years ago I received a slap in the face, and my assailant's still alive."

This made me intensely curious. "You never fought him?" I asked. "I suppose circumstances came between you?"

"I did fight him," Silvio replied. "And here's the memento of our duel."

Silvio got up and took from a cardboard box a braided red cap with a golden tassel (what the French call a *bonnet de police*). He put it on. It had a bullet hole within a few centimetres of the forehead.

"You're aware," continued Silvio, "that I served in the —— regiment of hussars. You know my temperament: I'm used to coming first, but as a young man that was my passion. In our day it was fashionable to be rowdy: I was the rowdiest chap in the army. We took pride in drunkenness: I outdrank the famous Burtsóv, whom Denís Davýdov celebrated.* In our regiment duels took place constantly: in every one I was either a witness or an active party.

My comrades idolized me; but the regimental commanders, who kept changing all the time, regarded me as a plague beyond remedy.

"I was quietly (or not so quietly) revelling in my reputation, when there joined our ranks a young man of rich and illustrious family (I'd rather not name him). Never in my life had I encountered such a well-favoured and brilliant chap! Just imagine: youth, brains, good looks, the most outrageous high spirits, the most reckless bravery, a resonant surname, money beyond his reckoning or his ability to spend – just think what an impact he must have made among us. My supremacy was shaken. Mesmerized by my reputation, he made as if to seek my friendship, but I treated him coldly, and he distanced himself from me without regret. I came to hate him. His successes in the regiment and in female company reduced me to utter desperation. I began to pick quarrels with him; he responded to my epigrams with epigrams that always seemed to me cleverer and sharper than my own, and that were in fact incomparably funnier. His were jokes, but mine were slanders. Finally, one day there was a ball at a Polish landowner's: seeing that he was the object of attention from all the ladies, but especially the hostess herself, with whom I was having an affair, I whispered in his ear some piece of coarse vulgarity. Incensed, he slapped me on the face. We reached for our swords; ladies swooned; people pulled us apart; so that very night we rode off to fight.

"By now it was first light. I stood at the designated spot with my three seconds. With inexpressible impatience I awaited my opponent. The spring sun rose, and it began to feel hot. I caught sight of him in the distance. He came on foot, his tunic slung over his sabre, accompanied by a single second. We went to meet him. He approached, holding his peaked cap full of wild cherries. The seconds measured us out twelve paces. I was to fire first; but the churning of spite within me was so violent that I could not rely on the steadiness of my arm; so, to give myself time to cool down, I tried to cede the first shot to him. My opponent would not agree. It was decided to cast lots: the winning number went to him, Fortune's perpetual favourite. He took aim and shot me through the cap. It was my turn. His life was now in my hands. I eyed him avidly, trying to discern the smallest shadow of disquiet. He stood within pistol range, picking ripe cherries from his cap and spitting the stones out at me.* His nonchalance enraged me. 'What good is it to me,' I thought, 'to rob him of life, when he sets no value by it at all?' A malicious thought flashed through my mind. I lowered my pistol.

"'You're evidently not ready to die just yet,' I said to him. 'You're enjoying your breakfast; I should hate to interrupt you.'

"'You're not interrupting me at all,' he retorted; 'fire, by all means. It's up to you, though. You've still your shot left; I'm always at your disposal.'

"I turned to the seconds and announced that I wasn't minded to fire for now; and with that the duel ended.

"I resigned my commission and came away to this little place. Since then not a day has passed without my thinking of revenge. Now my time has come…"

Silvio took out of his pocket the letter he had received that morning and gave it to me to read. Someone (evidently his agent) had written to him from Moscow that a "well-known personage" had announced his engagement to a beautiful young lady.

"You realize," said Silvio, "who this 'well-known personage' is. I'm off to Moscow. Let's see if he accepts death on the eve of his wedding as coolly as he once awaited it over the cherries!"

With those words Silvio stood up, threw the cap on the ground and began to pace up and down the room, like a caged tiger. I had listened to him without reacting. Strange, contradictory feelings unsettled me.

The servant entered and announced that the horses were ready. Silvio clasped my hand firmly; we embraced. He took his seat in the conveyance alongside two trunks, one holding the pistols and the second his other belongings. We said goodbye once again, and the horses galloped off.

CHAPTER 2

SOME YEARS PASSED, and private circumstances obliged me to take up residence on a meagre little estate in X district. Busy as I was with managing the property, I continued quietly to pine for my old boisterous and carefree existence. What I found most difficult was getting used to spending autumn and winter evenings in complete solitude. I still managed somehow to drag out the time till dinner, chatting with the village elder, riding round the fields or inspecting new projects; but as soon as it began to get dark, I had absolutely no idea what to do with myself. The few books that I found beneath cupboards or in the storeroom I had learnt by heart. Kirílovna, the housekeeper, had told me again and again all the folk tales that she could recollect; the peasant women's songs depressed me. I nearly took to hard liquor, but that made my head ache; and, truth to tell, I took fright at becoming a drunkard from sorrow – that is, the sorriest of drunkards! – many specimens of which I could see in our district. Nearby I had no neighbours at all, apart from two or three of these sorry fellows, whose discourse consisted mostly of burps and groans. Solitude was more bearable than that.

Four and a half kilometres away lay a wealthy property belonging to Countess B——; but only a manager lived there. The Countess had visited her property once, in the first year of her marriage, but had not stayed more than a month. Nevertheless, in the second spring of my hermit-like existence the rumour got around that the Countess and her husband were coming to their estate for the summer. They arrived, in fact, at the beginning of June.

The arrival of a wealthy neighbour is a momentous occasion for country-dwellers. Landowners and their servants talk of it for a couple of months beforehand and for three years afterwards. On me too, I admit, news of the advent of a young and pretty neighbour had a strong impact. I burned with impatience to set eyes on her; and so, on the first Sunday after her arrival, I set out after dinner for the village of —— to pay my respects to Their Excellencies, as their closest neighbour and most obedient servant.

A footman conducted me to the Count's study and went off himself to announce me. The spacious study was furnished with all imaginable luxury. Bookcases stood around the walls, a bronze bust on each. The marble fireplace was surmounted by a large mirror. The floor was covered with green felt and spread with rugs. I had grown unused to luxury in my wretched hideaway, and it was long now since I had encountered the wealth of others, so I grew embarrassed and somewhat nervous as I awaited the Count, like a petitioner from the provinces awaiting a minister's appearance. The doors opened, and in came a handsome-looking man of about thirty-two. The Count came up to me with an open and friendly expression; I tried to regain courage and was about to voice my respects, but he forestalled me. We sat down. His conversation, amiable and unconstrained, soon dispelled my shyness and inhibition; I was already beginning to recover my normal demeanour, when all at once the Countess entered, and I was seized with greater confusion than ever. She was indeed a beautiful woman. The Count introduced me; I wanted to appear relaxed, but the more at ease I tried to look the more awkward I felt. To allow me time to compose myself and get used to new company, they began to chat between themselves, treating me without ceremony like a good neighbour. Meanwhile I began to walk to and fro, inspecting the books and pictures. I am no picture buff, but one attracted my attention. It portrayed a view of Switzerland, but what struck me about it was not the artistry, but the fact that the canvas had been pierced by two bullets, one above the other.

"There's a good shot," I said, turning to the Count.

"Yes," he replied, "a quite remarkable shot. And do you shoot well?" he went on.

"Passably," I answered, pleased that the conversation had at last touched on a subject close to me. "I won't miss a playing card at thirty paces – with pistols I'm used to, of course."

"Really?" said the Countess, with an expression of great interest. "And would you, my dear, hit a card at thirty paces?"

"We'll have a go sometime," the Count replied. "In my heyday I didn't shoot badly; but it's now four years since I handled a pistol."

"Oh," I remarked, "in that case I'll lay a bet that Your Excellency won't hit a card even at twenty paces. The pistol requires daily practice. That I know from experience. In our regiment I was regarded as one of the best marksmen. Once I wasn't able to use a pistol for a whole month. Mine were under repair. What do you suppose, Your Excellency? The next time I came to shoot after that, I missed a bottle at twenty-five paces four times running. We had a captain, a witty, entertaining fellow; he happened to be there and said to me: 'It's clear, brother, that you can't bear to waste a bottle.' No, Your Excellency, it doesn't do to drop your practice, or you'll lose your aim straight away. The best marksman I've ever met used to shoot every day, at least three times before dinner. That was as regular for him as a tot of vodka."

The Count and Countess were glad that I had started talking.

"And how well did he shoot?" the Count asked me.

"Well, here's how well, Your Excellency: as soon as he saw a fly landing on the wall – you're laughing, Countess? By God, it's true! He'd see a fly and shout: 'Kuzka, pistol!' Then Kuzka would bring him a loaded pistol. Bang, he'd go, and smash the fly into the wall."

"That's amazing!" said the Count. "And what was his name?"

"Silvio, Your Excellency."

"Silvio!" cried the Count, leaping from his seat. "You knew Silvio?"

"I certainly did, Your Excellency. We were friends. In our regiment he was accepted as one of us, our comrade. But it's now five years since I've heard anything of him. So Your Excellency knew him too?"

"Knew him, yes, very much so. He didn't tell you?... No, I don't suppose he did. He didn't tell you about one quite bizarre incident?"

"Not the slap in the face, Your Excellency, that he received from some playboy at a ball?"

"And did he ever tell you the playboy's name?"

"No, Your Excellency, he never said... Ah, Your Excellency!" I continued, guessing the truth. "Forgive me... I didn't know... It surely wasn't you?..."

"Indeed it was," replied the Count, looking thoroughly disconcerted. "And the bullet-holed picture is a memento of our final encounter."

"Agh, my dear," said the Countess, "for God's sake, say no more; I dread to listen."

"No," rejoined the Count: "I shall tell all. He knows how I insulted his friend: so let him learn how Silvio took his revenge on me."

The Count pulled me up an armchair, and it was with the keenest interest that I heard the following story:

"Five years ago I got married. The first month, 'the honeymoon' as the English say, I spent here, on this estate. It's to this house I owe the best moments of my life, and one of my grimmest memories.

"We were out riding together one evening. My wife's mount became a bit fractious: she grew frightened, gave me the reins and returned home on foot. I rode ahead. Outside the house I saw a travelling conveyance. They told me there was a man sitting in the drawing room who didn't want to give his name, but had simply said he had business with me. I entered this room and saw in the gloom a man unshaven and covered in dust. He was standing here by the fireplace. I went up to him, trying to place his features.

"'Don't you recognize me, Count?' he said in a faltering voice.

"'Silvio!' I cried, and I confess that I felt my hair suddenly standing on end.

"'Precisely,' he continued. 'I'm owed a shot, and I've come to put my pistol to use. Are you ready?'

"His pistol was projecting from his side pocket. I measured out twelve paces, and took my stand there in the corner, asking him to shoot quickly, before my wife returned. He took his time, and asked for lights. They brought candles. I shut the doors, gave orders for no one to come in, and again asked him to shoot. He pulled out the pistol and took aim... I counted the seconds... I was thinking of her... Dreadful, the minute that passed! Silvio lowered his arm. 'A pity the pistol isn't loaded with cherry stones,' he said. 'A bullet's so heavy. I'm thinking all the time that in our case it's not a duel but murder: I'm not used to firing at one who's unarmed. Let's begin again and draw lots for who's to shoot first.'

"My head was in a whirl. I don't remember agreeing... At length we loaded a second pistol; we rolled up two bits of paper, and he placed them in the cap that I had once holed. Again I drew the first number.

"'You're devilish lucky, Count,' he said, with a smirk I'll never forget.

"I don't understand what had come over me and how he could have made me do it... but – I fired and hit that picture."

The Count pointed to the picture with the bullet holes: his face was burning like a fire; the Countess was paler than her handkerchief; I couldn't suppress an exclamation.

"I'd fired," the Count went on, "and, thank God, had missed. Then Silvio... at that moment he was terrifying indeed... Silvio began to aim at me. Suddenly the doors opened, Masha ran in and threw herself around my neck with a shriek. Her presence quite restored my courage.

"'Dearest,' I said to her, 'don't you see that we're just having some fun? You're so frightened over nothing! Go and drink a glass of water, then come back and I'll introduce to you an old friend and colleague.'

"Masha couldn't yet believe all this. 'Tell me: is what my husband's saying true?' she said, turning to the glowering Silvio. 'Is it true that the two of you are just having fun?'

"'He's always having fun, Countess,' Silvio replied to her. 'He once slapped me in the face for fun; he shot this cap of mine through for fun; and he's just missed me for fun. Now *I* want to have a bit of fun too.'

"With these words he was about to take aim at me… in front of her! Masha threw herself at his feet.

"'Get up, Masha, it's shameful!' I shouted in fury. 'But you, sir, will you stop playing games at a poor woman's expense? Are you going to shoot, or not?'

"'I'm not,' replied Silvio. 'I'm satisfied: I've seen your consternation, your fear; I've forced you to shoot at me. For me that's enough. You won't forget me. I leave you to your conscience.'

"With this he was about to go, but he stopped in the doorway, eyed the picture that I'd holed, took a shot at it almost without aiming, and disappeared. My wife lay in a faint; my people didn't dare to stop him but stared at him in terror. He went out onto the steps, summoned his coachman and drove off before I could come to my senses."

The Count fell silent. That is how I learnt the end of the story, whose beginning had once so astonished me. Its protagonist I never met again. They say that Silvio led a detachment of Hetaerists during Alexander Ypsilantis' uprising and was killed at the battle of Skulyány.*

The Blizzard*

O'er the hills the horses speed;
through deep snows they battle...
till, just there beside the road,
looms a lonely chapel.
....
All at once a blizzard strikes,
snowflakes densely flying;
raven wheels above the sleigh,
black-winged, harshly crying;
fateful croak forewarns of grief!
Steeds race on affrighted,
manes a-bristling, straining eyes
through the murk, keen-sighted...
*— Zhukóvsky**

A T THE END OF 1811 – a memorable period for us –
there lived on his estate of Nenarádovo the kindly Gavríla
Gavrílovich R—. He was famed throughout the district for hospitality and friendliness. Neighbours drove round to him all
the time for a bite to eat, for something to drink, for a game of
Boston with his wife Praskóvya Petróvna at five copecks a time,*
and (in some cases) for a glance at their young daughter Márya
Gavrílovna, a slim and pale girl of seventeen. She was seen as a
wealthy match, and there were many who marked her out for
themselves or their sons.

26

Márya Gavrílovna had been brought up on French novels and was therefore in love. Her choice had fallen on an impecunious subaltern in the regular army who was currently on leave on his estate. It goes without saying that the young man burned with an equal passion and that his beloved's parents, having noticed the couple's mutual attachment, forbade their daughter even to think of him and made him less welcome than a superannuated court clerk.

Our lovers wrote each other letters and met privately each day in a pine grove or by an old chapel. There they swore each other eternal love, bewailed their lot and made all kinds of plans. Out of this correspondence and discussion they reached (very naturally) the following conclusion: "If we're unable to draw breath apart from each other, and if heartless parents are determined to block our happiness, then why can't we go ahead regardless?" It goes without saying that this happy thought occurred first to the young man and that it greatly appealed to Márya Gavrílovna's romantic imagination.

Winter arrived and curtailed their rendezvous; but the correspondence became all the livelier. In every letter Vladímir Nikoláyevich begged her to give herself up to him, marry him secretly, go into hiding for a while, and then throw herself at the feet of her parents, who were bound in the end to be moved by the lovers' heroic steadfastness and suffering and were sure to say to them: "Children, come into our arms!"

Márya Gavrílovna hesitated for a long time. Most schemes for elopement were rejected. Finally she consented: on a prearranged day she was to refuse supper and retire to her room on the excuse of a headache. Her maid was in on the plot: they were both to go out into the garden by the back porch; beyond the garden they would find a sleigh ready; they would get into it and drive the five kilometres from Nenarádovo to the village of Zhádrino, straight to the church, where Vladímir would be waiting for them.

The night before the decisive day Márya Gavrílovna did not sleep at all. She sorted her things out, bundled up her dresses and underwear, and wrote one long letter to a sentimental young lady friend and another to her parents. She bade them farewell in the most touching terms, blamed her escapade on the overpowering strength of her passion, and ended by declaring that she would count it the happiest moment of her life when she might throw herself at her beloved parents' feet. She sealed both letters with a Tula-ware seal, engraved with two flaming hearts and an appropriate motto, then threw herself onto the bed just before daybreak and began to doze. Even so, dreadful dreams kept waking her every instant. Sometimes it seemed to her that, just as she was boarding the sleigh to ride to the wedding, her father would stop her, drag her at agonizing speed through the snow and throw her down into a dark and bottomless cavern... and she was plunging headlong in inexpressible despair. Sometimes she saw Vladímir lying on the grass, pale and covered in blood; he was dying, but kept begging her in a piercing voice to marry him quickly... Other horrific and idiotic visions passed before her one after another. Finally she got up, even paler than usual, and with a genuine headache. Her father and mother noticed her distress: their gentle solicitude and incessant enquiries – "What's the trouble, Masha? Surely you're ill, Masha?" – tore her heart. She tried to reassure them and appear cheerful, but could not. Evening came. She was crushed by the thought that this was the last day she was spending among her family. Hardly alive now, she kept inwardly bidding farewell to all the people, all the objects that surrounded her. Supper was served. Her heart began to pound. In a trembling voice she announced that she did not want any supper and began to say goodnight to her father and mother; they gave her a kiss and blessed her in their usual way; she nearly wept. On reaching her room, she collapsed into an armchair and dissolved into tears. The maid urged her to calm herself and be brave. All was ready. In half an hour Masha was to leave for ever her parental home, her room, the quiet life of an unmarried girl... Outside there was a blizzard; the wind howled, the shutters shook and rattled; it all seemed to her menacing, portending grief. Soon the whole household grew quiet and fell asleep. Masha wrapped herself in a shawl, threw a warm cloak over her shoulders, took her travelling case in her hand and went out onto the back porch. The servant came behind her with two bundles. They went down into the garden. The blizzard was not abating; the wind blew in her face, as though striving to halt the errant girl. They made it to the end of the garden with a struggle. The sleigh was waiting for them on the road. The horses, feeling the cold, would not stand still; Vladímir's coachman kept going back and forth in front of the shafts, holding the restless animals back. He helped the young lady and her maid take their seats and stow the case and bundles; then he seized the reins and the horses flew off. So, having entrusted the young lady to the care of fate and to the skill of coachman Teryóshka, let us turn to our lovesick young man.

Vladímir had been riding about the whole day. In the morning he had been to the priest at Zhádrino and had with difficulty secured his cooperation. Then he had set off to find witnesses among the local landowners. The first one he came to, a forty-year-old retired cornet called Dravin, had consented with alacrity. This adventure, he kept declaring, reminded him of the old days and of escapades in the hussars. He persuaded Vladímir to stay with him for lunch and assured him that there would be no problem finding another couple of witnesses. In fact, directly after lunch two visitors turned up: the land surveyor Shmit, in whiskers and spurs, and the local police chief's son, a lad of sixteen who had recently enlisted with the uhlans. They not only accepted Vladímir's proposal, but even pledged their willingness to lay down their lives for him. Vladímir embraced them delightedly and rode off home to make ready.

Dusk had long fallen. Vladímir dispatched his trusty Teryóshka to Nenarádovo with the troika and with instructions that were detailed and explicit; for himself he ordered a small one-horse sledge to be harnessed, and he set out for Zhádrino alone, without a driver, a couple of hours before Márya Gavrílovna was due to arrive there. He knew the road well: it was only a twenty-minute drive.

But hardly had Vladímir left the area for the open country when the wind rose and blew up such a snowstorm that he could see nothing. Within moments the road was buried; the landscape disappeared in a dense yellowish fog full of swirling white snow-flakes; sky and earth merged. Vladímir found himself on rough terrain and tried in vain to get back onto the road; the horse was floundering and all the time kept careering into snowdrifts and plunging into hollows; the sledge kept turning over. Vladímir's one concern was not to lose his bearings. But after what seemed to him more than half an hour he had still not reached Zhádrino Wood. Another ten minutes or so went by – and still no sight of the wood. Vladímir was riding across open country cut by deep gullies; the blizzard did not abate; the sky did not clear. The horse began to tire, and Vladímir streamed with sweat, despite being repeatedly up to his waist in snow.

At length he realized he had been riding in the wrong direction. He halted: he started thinking, racking his brain, working things out, and he convinced himself that he should have turned to the right. He set off to the right. His horse could scarcely walk. Vladímir had already been travelling for more than an hour. Zhádrino could not be far. But he rode and rode, and there was no end to the open country. It was all snowdrifts and gullies; the sledge was always overturning, and he was always righting it. Time was passing; Vladímir began to be seriously worried.

At last something black started to appear on one side. Vladímir turned that way. As he came near he saw a wood. "Thank

God," he thought, "it's close now." He started riding around the wood, hoping at any time to reach the road he knew or to come round to the other side: Zhádrino lay directly beyond it. He soon found a road and drove deep in among trees stripped bare by winter. There was shelter here from the raging wind; the road was smooth; the horse recovered; and Vladímir was reassured.

But on and on he rode, and there was no Zhádrino to be seen; the wood was endless. Vladímir realized with horror that he had strayed into an unknown forest. Desperation overwhelmed him. He gave the horse a blow; the wretched animal broke into a trot, but soon started to flag and, within a quarter of an hour, for all poor Vladímir's efforts, took to walking.

Gradually the trees started thinning out, and Vladímir emerged from the forest: there was no Zhádrino to be seen. It must have been about midnight. Tears streamed from his eyes; he rode on recklessly. The weather quietened; the storm clouds parted; in front of him lay a level expanse covered in an undulating white carpet. It was a clearish night. He saw close by a small hamlet made up of four or five farmhouses. Vladímir drove towards it. At the first hut he jumped from the sledge, ran up to a window and began to knock. After several minutes a wooden shutter was drawn up and an old man poked his grey beard out.

"What d'ye want?"

"Is Zhádrino far?"

"Zhádrino? Far?"

"Yes, yes! Is it far?"

"Not so far – it'll be around ten kilometres."

At this reply Vladímir clutched at his hair and stood motionless, like someone who had been sentenced to death.

"And where be you from?" the old man went on.

Vladímir was in no mood to answer questions. "Gaffer, can you get me horses for Zhádrino?"

"'Ow should we 'ave 'orses?" replied the old man.

"Well, can I at least take a guide? I'll pay as much as he wants."

"Wait," said the old man, lowering the shutter, "I'll send ye me son. 'E'll show ye the way."

Vladímir started waiting. Before a minute had passed he began to knock again. The shutter went up, the beard appeared.

"What d'ye want?"

"What about your son?"

"'E'll be out straight away. 'E's putting 'is boots on. Are ye cold? Come along in and warm yeself up a bit."

"No, thanks. Just send your son out quickly."

A door creaked; out came a lad with a heavy stick and walked off ahead, now pointing out the road, now searching for it, smothered as it was in snowdrifts.

"What's the time?" Vladímir asked him.

"It'll soon be daylight," the young peasant replied.

Vladímir said not a word more.

Cockerels were crowing and it was already light when they reached Zhádrino. The church was shut. Vladímir paid off the guide and drove to the priest's house. There was no troika of his outside. What news awaited him!

But let us return to the good gentry of Nenarádovo and take a look at what is going on there.

Nothing.

The old couple woke up and emerged into the drawing room. Gavríla Gavrílovich was in a nightcap and flannel jacket, Praskóvya Petróvna in a padded dressing gown. The samovar was brought in, and Gavríla Gavrílovich sent the young serving maid to find out from Márya Gavrílovna if she was well and how she had slept. The maid returned to announce that the young mistress had "slept badly", but she was "now feeling easier", and would "be in the drawing room in a moment". Indeed, the door opened, and Márya Gavrílovna came across to greet her papa and mamma.

"How's your head, Masha?" enquired Gavríla Gavrílovich.

"Better, Papa," Masha replied.

"It must have been the fumes from the stove yesterday, Masha," said Praskóvya Petróvna.

"Possibly, Mamma," Masha replied.

The day passed satisfactorily, but during the night Masha was taken ill. They sent to the town for a doctor. He arrived towards evening and found the patient delirious. A severe fever had developed, and the poor patient remained between life and death for two weeks.

No one in the house knew of the projected elopement. The letters she had written the day before had been burnt; her maid said nothing to anyone, for fear of the master and mistress's wrath. The priest, the retired cornet, the whiskered surveyor and the young uhlan had good reason for discretion. The coachman Teryóshka never spoke a needless word, even over a drink. So the half a dozen or more accomplices all kept the secret. Márya Gavrílovna blurted it out herself, however, during her protracted delirium; but her words were so garbled that her mother, who never left her bedside, could gather only that her daughter was desperately in love with Vladímir Nikoláyevich and that this love was probably the cause of her illness. She took counsel with her husband and with several neighbours, and they all ended up by concluding unanimously that "such must be Márya Gavrílovna's destiny", that "even on horseback you'll never outride Mr Right", that "poverty is no crime", that "it's the man you live with, not the money", and so on. Moral sayings are marvellously useful when we can think of little justification ourselves for what we want to do.

The daughter of the house, meanwhile, started to recover. It was long since Vladímir had put in an appearance at Gavríla Gavrílovich's. He had been frightened off by his usual reception. It was decided to send for him and tell him of his unlooked-for good fortune: consent for the marriage. But imagine the dismay of the owners of Nenarádovo when in reply to their invitation they received a half-crazed letter from him! He informed them that he would never set foot in their house and begged them to forget a wretch for whom death was the one remaining hope. A few days later they learnt that Vladímir had left for the army. That was in 1812.*

For a long time, while Masha was recuperating, no one dared tell her about this. She never mentioned Vladímir. Several months later, having come across his name in a list of those seriously wounded during distinguished service at Borodinó, she fell into a swoon, and people feared that her fever might return. Thank God, though, the swoon had no sequel.

Another sorrow supervened: Gavríla Gavrílovich passed away, leaving her heiress to all his property. But the inheritance was no consolation to her; she wholeheartedly shared the grief of poor Praskóvya Petróvna, and vowed that she would never part from her; together they left Nenarádovo, a place of sad memories, and drove off to live on the estate of ——.

Here too eligible suitors circled round the rich and charming girl; but she gave none of them the slightest cause for hope. Her mother sometimes urged her to choose herself a partner; Márya Gavrílovna would shake her head and fall into a reverie. Vladímir was no longer alive: he had died in Moscow on the eve of the city's occupation by the French. His memory seemed sacred to Masha; at any rate she treasured everything that could remind her of him: books he had once read, sketches he had made, music and verses he had copied out for her. None of this escaped the neighbours, who marvelled at her devotion and awaited with curiosity the hero whose destiny it would be finally to triumph over the pathetic loyalty of this virginal Artemisia.*

Meanwhile the war had come to its glorious end. Our regiments returned from abroad. People flocked to meet them. Bands played songs brought back from the campaign: 'Vive Henri-Quatre';* Tyrolean waltzes* and arias from *Joconde*.* Officers who had left for war as little more than boys came back grown men, matured in the smoke of battle and festooned with medals. Soldiers chatted cheerily among themselves, constantly seasoning their speech with German and French expressions. Unforgettable time! Time of glory and patriotism! How strongly did the Russian heart beat at the word *fatherland*! How joyful were the tears of reunion! How united we were in linking feelings of national pride with love for the Sovereign! And what a moment it was for him!

Women, Russian women, were then as they have been at no other time. Their habitual coolness vanished. Their enthusiasm was truly overwhelming when they greeted the victors with cries of *Hoorah!* – "and in the air they tossed their bonnets".* Which officer from that time would not acknowledge that he owed the Russian woman his best, most precious reward?...

At that brilliant period Márya Gavrílovna was living with her mother in —— province and missed the sight of both capitals celebrating the troops' homecoming. But in the districts and the countryside the general enthusiasm was perhaps even stronger. When an officer arrived in those parts it was a real triumph for him, and while he was around no lover in a civilian jacket stood a chance.

We were already commenting that, for all her unresponsiveness, Márya Gavrílovna was still, as before, besieged by suitors. But they all had to retreat when there arrived at her stronghold an invalided colonel of hussars, Burmín, with a cross of St George in his buttonhole, and an "intriguing pallor", as the young ladies of the area used to put it. He was around twenty-six years old. He had come to spend leave on his properties, which lay in the vicinity of Márya Gavrílovna's estate. Márya Gavrílovna showed a marked partiality for him. In his presence her normal pensiveness took on new animation. One could not say that she flirted with him, but a poet who observed her behaviour would have said:

Se amor non è, che dunque?...*

Burmín was indeed a most amiable young man. He possessed exactly the disposition that appeals to women: courteous and considerate, completely unaffected and amusingly indiscreet. His conduct towards Márya Gavrílovna was straightforward and unconstrained; but whatever she said or did, his attention, inwardly and outwardly, stayed fixed on her. He appeared to be of a quiet and modest nature, but rumour had it that he had once been a frightful tearaway – and this did him no harm in the mind of Márya Gavrílovna, who (like all young ladies there have ever been) was happy to excuse roguishness as evidence of a daring and spirited character.

But more than all else – more than his gentleness, more than his agreeable conversation, more than his "intriguing pallor", more than his bandaged arm – more than anything else, it was the young hussar's reserve that stirred her curiosity and imagination. She could not fail to acknowledge that he liked her a lot; probably he too, with his intelligence and experience, had already been able to observe her partiality for him – how come, then, that she had not yet seen him at her feet, not yet heard him declare himself? What held him back? Was it the timidity inseparable from true love? Was it pride? Or was it the teasing of a wily philanderer? It was a puzzle to her. After good thought she decided that timidity was the sole cause, and she made up her mind to embolden him by greater attentiveness and even, as opportunity allowed, by signs of affection. She was preparing a denouement that would be completely unexpected, and she awaited the moment for the romantic declaration with impatience. A secret of any kind always lies heavy on the female heart. Her strategy had the desired effect: at least, Burmín fell into such an abstraction, and his black eyes rested on Márya Gavrílovna with such fire, that the decisive moment seemed at hand. The neighbours were talking of the wedding as a deed already done, and the good Praskóvya Petróvna was rejoicing that her daughter had at last found herself a worthy bridegroom.

One day the old lady was sitting alone in the drawing room dealing cards for *grande patience*, when Burmín entered the room and immediately asked for Márya Gavrílovna.

"She's in the garden," replied the old lady. "Go and find her, and I'll wait for you here."

Burmín went, and the old lady crossed herself and thought: "Today, maybe, it'll all be settled."

Burmín found Márya Gavrílovna by the pond, under a willow tree, with a book in her hand and wearing a white dress – quite the novelette heroine. After initial enquiries, Márya Gavrílovna purposely stopped sustaining the conversation, thereby intensifying mutual embarrassment, from which the only possible escape would be through an abrupt and decisive declaration. And so it happened: Burmín, conscious of the difficulty of his position, declared that he had long been seeking an opportunity to open his heart to her and asked for a moment of her attention. Márya Gavrílovna closed her book and lowered her eyes to signal consent.

"I love you," said Burmín. "I love you passionately…" Márya Gavrílovna blushed and bent her head even lower. "I've acted unwisely: I've indulged a delightful habit, the habit of seeing and hearing you each day…" Márya Gavrílovna recalled Saint-Preux's opening letter.* "For too long now I've been resisting my fate. The memory of you, your dear, incomparable image, will from now on be my life's torment and my life's solace. But there's still a heavy duty left me to carry out – to disclose to you a dreadful secret and place between us an insurmountable barrier—"

"It has always existed," broke in Márya Gavrílovna animatedly. "I could never have been your wife…"

"I know," he answered her softly, "I know you were once in love, but death and three years of mourning… Good, dear Márya Gavrílovna, do not try to deprive me of my last consolation – the thought that you would have consented to bring me happiness, if only… Don't speak, for God's sake, don't speak. You're torturing me. Yes, I know, I sense that you would have been mine, but... I'm the unhappiest of creatures... I'm married!"

Márya Gavrílovna gave him a look of astonishment.

"I'm married," Burmín continued. "I've been married now for over three years, and I don't know who my wife is, or where she is, or whether I'm ever destined to meet her again!"

"What are you saying?" exclaimed Márya Gavrílovna. "How extraordinary this is! Go on; I'll tell you afterwards... but go on, I beg you."

"At the beginning of 1812," said Burmín, "I was hurrying to Vilna,* where our regiment was stationed. On one occasion I arrived at a post station late in the evening. I was about to order horses to be harnessed urgently, when suddenly a frightful blizzard got up, and the postmaster and coachmen advised me to sit it out. I listened to them, but an incomprehensible restlessness came over me; it was even as if someone was driving me on. Meanwhile the blizzard didn't die down. I couldn't hold out, I ordered the horses to be reharnessed, and I set off into the raging storm. The coachman's idea was to drive along the river, which should have shortened our route by three kilometres. The banks were buried in snow. The coachman drove past the place for turning back onto the road, so we found ourselves in an unknown area. The storm had not subsided; I saw a small light and gave orders to drive there. We reached a village; the light was coming from a wooden church. The church was open, and several sledges were standing behind the fence. People were pacing up and down the porch. 'This way! This way!' shouted several voices. I ordered the coachman to drive up. 'In Heaven's name, where have you been loitering?' someone said to me. 'The bride's in a faint; the priest doesn't know what to do; we were all ready to ride home. Get out quickly!' I jumped from the sleigh in silence and entered the church, dimly lit by two or three candles. A girl was sitting on a stall in a dark corner of the church; another was rubbing her temples. 'Thank God,' said the second girl, 'you've arrived at long last. You've almost been the death of the young mistress.' The old priest came up to me and asked: 'Do you want to begin?' 'Begin, begin, Father,' I answered distractedly. They got the girl to her feet. She seemed to me not bad-looking… (Incomprehensible, unpardonable thoughtlessness!…) I took my stand beside her in front of the lectern; the priest was in a hurry; the three men and the maidservant were supporting the bride and preoccupied with her. The wedding was completed. 'Exchange kisses,' they told us. My wife turned her wan face towards me. I was about to kiss her… She shrieked: 'Aah! it's not him, not him!' and collapsed senseless. The witnesses stared at me, eyes aghast. I turned round, left the church without anyone trying to stop me, leapt into the sleigh and yelled: 'Go!'"

"Good God!" cried Márya Gavrílovna. "And you've no idea what happened to your poor wife?"

"No idea." replied Burmín. "I've no idea what the village where I got married was called; I can't remember which post station I'd set out from. At the time I saw so little importance in the wicked trick I'd played that, after leaving the church, I fell asleep and only woke up the next morning, three post stations farther on. The servant who was with me at the time died in the campaign, so I've no hope at all of finding the woman I trifled with so cruelly and who has now been so cruelly avenged."

"My God, my God!" said Márya Gavrílovna, grasping his hand. "So it was you! And you don't recognize me?"

Burmín turned pale... and threw himself at her feet...

The Undertaker*

> *Do we not see each day the graves*
> *and greying heads of frail humanity?*
> – Derzhávin*

T HE LAST OF UNDERTAKER Adrián Prókhorov's* posses-
sions had been loaded onto a hearse, and a scraggy pair
of horses had lumbered for a fourth time from Basmánnaya to
Nikítskaya Street,* where the undertaker was moving to with all
his household. After locking the premises he nailed a notice to
the gates announcing that the building was for sale or rent and set
out on foot for his new abode. As he approached the little yellow
house that had so long tickled his imagination and that he had at
last purchased for a tidy sum, the old undertaker was dismayed to
feel no joy in his heart. Crossing the unfamiliar threshold to find
his new dwelling in chaos, he heaved a sigh for the tumbledown
shack where for eighteen years everything had been arranged
in meticulous order; then he began scolding his two daughters
and the housekeeper for their sloth and set about helping them
himself. Soon order was established: the icon case with its icons,
the cupboard with its china, the table, couch and bed occupied
the corners assigned them in the back room; in the kitchen and
living room were stowed the proprietor's products – coffins of all

colours and sizes – plus cupboards of funerary hats, cloaks and torches. Over the gate a signboard had been put up depicting a plump cupid with a downturned torch in his hand, captioned: "Coffins, plain and fancy, sold and upholstered; also for hire; old ones repaired." The girls went off to their chamber; Adrián did a tour of his house, sat down by a small window and ordered a samovar to be heated.

The cultivated reader will be aware that both Shakespeare and Walter Scott portrayed their gravediggers as cheerful and jocular characters,* using the incongruity to make a deeper impact on our imagination. Out of respect for the truth we cannot follow their example; we are forced to acknowledge that our own undertaker's personality was entirely in keeping with his gloomy profession. Adrián Prókhorov was habitually morose and reserved. He hardly broke silence except to reprimand his daughters when he found them idly gaping out of the window at passers-by or to demand an exorbitant price for his goods from those unlucky enough (or, sometimes, fortunate enough) to have need of them. Accordingly, as Adrián sat at the window drinking his seventh cup of tea, he was, as normal, sunk in melancholy reflections. He was thinking of the torrential rain that had caught the funeral cortège of a retired brigadier a week ago at the very gate of the city. It had shrunk many of his cloaks and bent many of his hats out of shape. He foresaw unavoidable expense, since his ageing stock of funeral attire was getting into a pitiful state. He had been hoping to charge the damage up to old Tryúkhina, a shopkeeper's wife, who had been at death's door for a year or so. But Tryúkhina was dying in Razgulyáy,* and Prókhorov feared that her heirs, despite their promise, would not trouble to send for him at such a distance but hire the nearest contractor.

These musings were suddenly interrupted by three Masonic knocks on the door.*

"Who's there?" asked the undertaker.

The door opened, and into the room came a man instantly recognizable as a German artisan; he approached the undertaker with a cheerful look.

"Forgive me, dear neighbour," he said in that accented Russian that we still cannot hear without laughing – "forgive me for disturbing you... I wanted to make your acquaintance without delay. I'm a shoemaker; my name's Gottlieb Schulz, and I live across the street from you in that little house you can see from your windows. Tomorrow I'm celebrating my silver wedding, and I should like you and your young daughters to join me for a friendly meal."

The invitation was graciously accepted. The undertaker asked the shoemaker to sit down for a cup of tea and, thanks to Gottlieb Schulz's affable manner, they soon got into an amicable conversation.

"How's your business, good sir?" enquired Adrián.

"Agh," replied Schulz, "so-so. Can't complain – though, of course, my trade's not the same as yours. A live man can do without shoes, but a corpse can't live without a grave!"

"The absolute truth," commented Adrián. "Even so, if a live man can't afford shoes, then – sadly – he'll go around barefoot; but a dead beggar gets himself a grave for nothing."

Their conversation went on like this for some time. At length the shoemaker got up and said goodbye to the undertaker, repeating his invitation.

The next day, at exactly twelve o'clock, the undertaker and his daughters emerged from the small door of their newly purchased house and set off for the neighbour's.

In this instance I shall depart from the practice adopted by today's novelists: I shall refrain from describing Adrián Prókhorov's Russian caftan or Akulína and Dárya's European outfits. I do not, though, regard it out of place to remark that both girls had dressed up in the yellow hats and red shoes they kept for celebratory occasions.

The shoemaker's cramped little apartment was full of guests, mostly German artisans with their wives and apprentices. Russian officialdom was represented only by a watchman called Yurko, a Finn, who despite his humble status had managed to win the host's special regard. For twenty-five years he had served in his position with loyalty and honesty, like Pogorélsky's postman.* The conflagration of 1812 that had laid waste the tsars' ancient capital had also destroyed Yurko's yellow watchman's hut. But immediately after the enemy's expulsion there had appeared in its place a new greyish one, with little white Doric columns, and Yurko had again begun to march up and down outside it "with axe, in homespun battledress".*

Yurko was known to most of the Germans that lived near Nikítsky Gate: some of them had even had occasion to spend Sunday nights in his tutelage. Adrián immediately introduced himself to him, as someone who sooner or later might be useful to him, and when the party moved to the dining table they sat together. Mr and Mrs Schulz and their seventeen-year-old daughter Lottchen, though dining with the guests, served up the food and helped the cook pass it round. Beer flowed. Yurko ate enough for four; Adrián did no worse; his daughters made a show of their good manners; the conversation in German grew ever noisier. Suddenly the host called for attention and, uncorking a pitch-sealed bottle, proclaimed loudly in Russian: "To the health of my good Louisa!" The would-be champagne frothed up. The host tenderly kissed the fresh face of his forty-year-old companion, and the guests loudly drank good Louisa's health. "To the health of my dear guests!" pronounced the host, uncorking a second bottle, and the guests thanked him as they again drained their glasses. From now on toasts followed one after another: they drank the health of each guest individually; they drank the health of Moscow and of a good dozen little German towns; they drank the health of guilds in general and of each guild separately; they drank the health of master craftsmen and apprentices. Adrián drank with enthusiasm, and brightened up to the extent of proposing some facetious toast himself. Suddenly one of the guests, a stout baker, raised his glass and cried: "To the health of all those for whose good we work, *unserer Kundleute*!"* This toast, like all the others, was taken up rapturously and unanimously. The guests began bowing to each other, tailor to shoemaker, shoemaker to tailor, baker to both, everyone to the tailor, and so on. Amid all these mutual bowings Yurko turned to his neighbour and shouted out: "Well then, sir – drink to the health of your corpses!" Everyone burst out laughing, but the undertaker took offence and scowled. No one noticed; the guests went on drinking, and the church bells were already ringing for vespers when they got up from the table.

The guests departed late, and for the most part merry. The stout baker and the bookbinder, his face seemingly bound in red morocco leather,* took Yurko by the arms and led him off to his hut, complying thereby with the Russian saying "a debt's made good by payment". The undertaker came home drunk and angry.

"Well, really!" he kept arguing aloud. "How's my profession less honourable than the rest? Surely an undertaker's not akin to a hangman? What are they laughing at, the heathens? An undertaker's no Christmas clown, is he? I was meaning to invite them to a housewarming, treat them to a mountain of a feast; there'll be none of that now! Instead I'll invite the folk for whose good I work: true Christian corpses!"

"What are you on about, master?" asked the housekeeper, who was at that moment pulling off his shoes. "What's this nonsense you're talking? Cross yourself! Invite corpses to a housewarming? Abomination!"

"By God I will! I'll invite them," Adrián went on, "and for tomorrow. Do me the favour, dear patrons, of feasting with me tomorrow evening: I'll treat you to all that God has provided."

With these words the undertaker went off to bed and soon began to snore.

It was still dark outside when Adrián was awakened. The shop-keeper's wife Tryúkhina had died that very night, and a special messenger from her house manager had galloped to Adrián on horseback with the news. The undertaker tipped him ten copecks for vodka, quickly got dressed, took a cab and drove off to Razgulyáy. Police were already stationed at the dead woman's door, and tradespeople were stalking up and down, like ravens scenting a dead body. The deceased lay on a table, yellow as wax, but not yet disfigured by decay. Around her clustered relatives, neighbours and servants. All the windows were open; candles were burning; priests were reciting prayers. Adrián went up to Tryúkhina's nephew, a young shopkeeper in a fashionable frockcoat, assuring him that a coffin, candles, drapes and all appurtenances for a funeral would be supplied immediately and in thoroughly good order. The heir thanked him abstractedly, saying that he would not haggle over the price, but relied on the undertaker's good faith in everything. The undertaker, as was his habit, swore to God that he would not overcharge, exchanged a knowing look with the house manager and drove off to get on with the business. He spent the whole day driving from Razgulyáy to Nikítskaya and back; by evening he had arranged everything and set off home on foot, having dismissed his cab. It was a moonlit night. The undertaker reached the Nikítsky Gate without mishap. At the Church of the Ascension our friend Yurko stopped him and, recognizing the undertaker, wished him good night. It was late. The undertaker was already approaching his house when suddenly he thought he saw someone walking up to his gate, opening the small door and disappearing inside. "What might that mean?" thought Adrián. "Who has need of me now? Surely a thief hasn't got in? Surely boyfriends aren't visiting my silly girls? Little risk of that!" And the undertaker was already thinking of calling on his friend Yurko for help.

At that moment someone else came up to the small door and was about to enter but, seeing the proprietor running up, he stopped and doffed his tricorne hat. Adrián thought his face familiar but, flustered as he was, he didn't manage to get a proper look at him.

"I'm honoured by your visit," said Adrián, out of breath. "Do go in, please."

"Don't stand on ceremony, sir," replied the other in a muffled voice. "Go ahead yourself; show your guests the way!"

Adrián had never had time for standing on ceremony. The small door was unlocked; he went upstairs, with the other behind him. It seemed to Adrián that there were people walking around in his rooms.

"What devilish business is this?" he thought and made haste to enter... then his legs gave way. The room was full of corpses. Through the window the moon illuminated their faces, yellow and livid, their sunken mouths, their dark and half-closed eyes, their jutting noses... Aghast, Adrián recognized in them people whose burials he had organized, and in the guest that had entered with him he saw the brigadier whose funeral had taken place in pouring rain. All of them, men and women, gathered round the undertaker with bows and greetings, save for one pauper recently buried free of charge, who, in embarrassment and shame at his rags, kept his distance and stood meekly in a corner. The rest were all respectably dressed; deceased ladies in bonnets and ribbons; official corpses in uniforms but with beards unshaven; tradesmen in festive caftans.

"You see, Prókhorov," said the brigadier in the name of the whole distinguished company, "we've all come up for your party; the only ones left at home are those who are already incapacitated, completely decomposed or left with bones and no skin – but even so there was one who couldn't hold himself back – he so much wanted to visit you…"

At that moment a short skeleton pushed its way through the crowd and walked up to Adrián. The skull grinned ingratiatingly at the undertaker. Scraps of bright-green and red material and old canvas hung on him here and there as on a post, and the bones of his legs knocked around in his oversize jackboots like little pestles on mortars.

"You don't recognize me, Prókhorov?" said the skeleton. "Do you remember a retired guards sergeant Pyótr Petróvich Kurílkin, the one you sold your first coffin to in 1799 – a pinewood one when it should have been oak?"

With these words the dead man stretched out his arms for a bony embrace – but Adrián, collecting himself with an effort, screamed and pushed him away. Pyótr Petróvich reeled, fell and shattered completely. A murmur of indignation arose among the corpses. They all took the part of their abused comrade and laid into Adrián with protests and threats; and the master of the house, poor man, deafened by their shouts and nearly crushed, lost control of himself, collapsed on top of the retired sergeant's bones and passed out.

The sun had long been shining on the bed where the undertaker lay. At last he opened his eyes and saw in front of him his housekeeper blowing the samovar into life. Adrián recalled in terror all the previous day's events. Confused images of Tryúkhina, the brigadier and Sergeant Kurílkin crowded into his mind. He waited in silence for the woman to start a conversation with him and explain the sequel to the night's happenings.

"You've truly overslept, Adrián Prókhorovich, master," said Axínya, offering him his dressing gown. "Our neighbour the tailor called to see you, and the local watchman dropped in to tell you it's the police inspector's name day today, but you were happily dozing away, and we didn't want to wake you."

"And did people come from the Tryúkhina woman who passed away?"

"'Passed away'? She's not dead, is she?"

"You stupid woman! Wasn't it you that helped me arrange her funeral yesterday?"

"What's up with you, master? Have you lost your senses? Or haven't you got over last night's drinking yet? What's this about a funeral yesterday? You were enjoying good food all day at the German's; you got back drunk, fell into bed – yes, and slept till now, when the bells have already rung for Mass."

"Really?" said the undertaker, much relieved.

"For sure it's so," replied the woman.

"Well, in that case hurry up with tea, and call the daughters."

The Postmaster*

*...Just a collegiate registrar**
(but, at the post station, a tsar!)
– Prince Vyázemsky*

W HO HASN'T CURSED A POSTMASTER? Who hasn't
wrangled with them? Who hasn't, in a moment of anger,
demanded of them the dreaded book, in which to register a pointless complaint about high-handedness, rudeness or negligence?
Who doesn't consider them the dregs of humanity, equivalent
to those unlamented clerks of old Muscovy, or at least to the
brigands of Murom?*

Let's be fair, though: let's try to put ourselves in their position, and maybe we'll form a much kindlier assessment of them.
What is a postmaster? A veritable martyr of the fourteenth grade,
safeguarded by rank alone from beatings – and that's not always
so (I appeal to my readers' conscience)! What is the job of this
"tsar", as Prince Vyázemsky jokingly calls him? Is it not in truth
a sentence of hard labour? No peace by day or night! It's on the
postmaster that a traveller takes out all the pent-up frustrations
of a tedious journey: intolerable weather, filthy road, stubborn
coachman, horses that won't pull – they're the postmaster's fault.
On entering his impoverished dwelling, the traveller glares at him

like a foe. Fine if he can quickly rid himself of his uninvited guest; but if there happen to be no horses?… Good God – what abuse, what threats pour down on his head! In rain and sleet he has to run from stable to stable. In storm and midwinter frost he retires to the porch, just to get a moment's break from being hectored and jostled by an irate customer. A general rides up; the trembling postmaster allocates him his last two teams of three, including the one for the government messenger. The general drives on, without so much as a thank-you. Five minutes later – bell jangles!… – and a courier slaps his road pass down on the desk!… Once we look at all this properly our annoyance will give way to heartfelt compassion.

A few words more: for all of twenty years I've travelled over Russia in every direction. I know nearly all the post routes; I know several generations of coachmen; there are few postmasters I don't recognize, few I haven't had dealings with. I hope shortly to publish a fascinating travelogue; in the meantime I shall just say that the public has been given an utterly false picture of the fraternity of postmasters. Much maligned as they are, postmasters are generally peaceable folk, obliging by nature, fond of company, unassuming and not unduly grasping. From their conversation (misguidedly spurned by travelling gentry) one can gather much that's interesting and instructive. For myself, I confess I prefer their gossip to the talk of any official of the sixth rank* travelling on business of state.

It will readily be understood that I have friends among the honoured fraternity of postmasters. There is one in particular whose memory I cherish. Circumstances once brought us together, and it's he I mean now to talk to you about, good readers.

In May 1816 I happened to be travelling across —— province, by a post road that's now been abolished. I was of low rank; I was riding post and paying the rate for just two horses. Because of this postmasters didn't put themselves out for me, and I often had to fight to get what I considered my entitlement. Being young and hot-tempered, I used to get angry at a postmaster's meanness and small-mindedness when he harnessed up the three-horse team prepared for me to the carriage of some high-ranking squire. For a long time, too, I was unable to stomach being passed over by a pedantic lackey serving dishes at a governor's dinner.* Now I see both as how things are. Where should we be, indeed, if the customary and convenient rule "Rank, respect rank!" were replaced by an alternative – say, "Brains, respect brains!"? What disputes there'd be! And who would servants offer food to first? But I return to my story.

It was a hot day. Three kilometres from the —— post station it started to rain, and within a minute a downpour had soaked me to the skin. When I arrived at the station my first priority was a quick change of clothes, and the second to order myself tea.

"Hey, Dunya!" shouted the postmaster. "Get the samovar ready and fetch some cream."

At these words a girl of about fourteen came out from behind a partition and ran off into the porch. I was struck by her attractiveness.

"Is that your daughter?" I asked the postmaster.

"Yes, sir, my daughter," he replied with an expression of pleasure and pride. "And so intelligent, so alert, just like her poor mother."

He then got on with registering my road pass, and I occupied myself with inspecting the small pictures that decorated his humble but tidy little dwelling. They illustrated the story of the prodigal son.* In the first a venerable old man in night cap and dressing gown is seeing off an impatient lad who hurriedly accepts his blessing and a bag of money. The next was a vivid portrayal of the youngster's dissolute behaviour: he sits at a table surrounded by false friends and loose women. Further on, the lad, in rags and tricorne hat, money now gone, is feeding swine and sharing their repast; his face depicts deep sorrow and remorse. Pictured last was his return to his father: the kindly old man, in the same nightcap and dressing gown, runs out to meet him; the prodigal son is on his knees; in the background a cook is killing the fatted calf; and the elder brother is asking some servants the reason for such celebrations. Beneath each picture I read apt verses in German. All this has stayed in my memory till now, as too have the pots of flowering balsamine, the bed with coloured hangings and all the other objects then around me. I can see, as though today, the master of the house himself, a man of about fifty, fresh-faced and healthy, and his long green coat with three medals on faded ribbons.

I had not had time to settle up with my elderly driver before Dunya returned with the samovar. The little flirt observed at second glance the impression she had made on me; she lowered her large blue eyes; I started conversing with her, and she answered me with no shyness at all, like a girl who has seen the world. I offered her father a glass of punch,* to Dunya I handed a cup of tea, and the three of us began chatting as though we had known each other for ever.

The horses had long been ready, but I was still reluctant to part with the postmaster and his daughter. At length I bade them goodbye; the father wished me a good journey, and the daughter saw me to the carriage. In the porch I stopped and asked permission to give her a kiss; Dunya consented… I can count many kisses "from when I've had an interest in such things",* but none has left me with a memory so lasting and so delightful.

A few years went by; then circumstances brought me by the same post road to the same parts. I remembered the old postmaster's daughter, and was looking forward to seeing her again. But then it occurred to me that the old postmaster might have been replaced, and Dunya was probably married by now. The thought that one or other might have died also flashed through my mind, and I approached the —— post station with foreboding.

The horses halted at the little post house. On entering the room I immediately recognized the pictures depicting the story of the prodigal son; the table and bed stood in their former positions; but there were no longer flowers on the window sills; and the whole place gave an impression of decrepitude and shabbiness. The postmaster was asleep under a sheepskin coat; my arrival awakened him, and he sat up... It was the same Simeón Vyrin* – but how he'd aged! While he was getting on with registering my road pass, I observed his grey hair, the wrinkles on his long-unshaven face, his bent back – and I was amazed how three or four years could have transformed a stalwart fellow into a frail old man.

"Do you recognize me?" I asked him. "We're old acquaintances, you and I."

"Possibly," he replied grumpily. "It's a main road here; I've had plenty of travellers passing through."

"Is your Dunya well?" I went on.

The old man frowned. "God only knows," he answered.

"So she's married, I suppose?" I said.

The old man pretended he'd not heard my question and went on reading my road pass in an undertone. I ceased my questions and ordered a pot of tea. Curiosity was beginning to needle me, and I hoped that some punch would loosen my old friend's tongue.

I was not mistaken: the old man did not refuse the glass I offered. I noted that the rum cleared away his ill humour. Over the second glass he became chatty. He remembered me – or put on an appearance of doing so – and I heard from him a story that, in the telling, engrossed and moved me deeply.

"So you knew my Dunya?" he began. "Yes, yes, who didn't know her? Ah, Dunya, Dunya! What a lass she was! In those days whoever drove by – they'd all pay compliments, no one found fault. Ladies used to give her presents – some hankies, others earrings.

Gentlemen travellers used to stop by on purpose, supposedly to have lunch or dinner, but really just to take a longer look at her. In those days the gentry, be they ever so angry, would quieten down when she was near and chat politely to me. Would you believe it, sir: government messengers and couriers would chatter away with her for half an hour on end. She kept the place going, she did: any clearing up, any cooking there was to be done, she coped with it all. And as for me, old fool, I couldn't see enough of her, couldn't have enough of her company. Didn't I love my Dunya, didn't I dote on her? And wasn't she happy here? But no, you'll never get God to keep trouble away; you'll never escape what's fated."

And he went on to tell me his sad story in detail.

Three years earlier, one winter evening, when the postmaster was ruling lines in a new register and his daughter was hemming a dress behind the partition, a troika drove up, and a wayfarer in a Circassian cap and military greatcoat, muffled in a scarf, entered the room and demanded horses. All the horses were out on the road. Told of this, the traveller began to raise his voice, and his whip; but Dunya, who was used to such scenes, ran out from behind the partition and disarmingly addressed the wayfarer with the question: wouldn't he like something to eat? Dunya's appearance had its usual effect. The traveller's anger passed; he agreed to wait for the horses and ordered himself some supper. Once he had doffed his shaggy, wet hat, unwrapped his scarf and pulled off his greatcoat, the traveller emerged as a handsome young hussar with a neat black moustache. He made himself at home with the postmaster and began to converse jovially with him and his daughter. Supper was served. Meanwhile some horses arrived, and the postmaster ordered them to be harnessed immediately to the traveller's sleigh without being fed. On returning, however, he found the young man lying on a bench, almost unconscious: he'd had a bad turn; his head had started aching; it was impossible to drive on... What was to be done? The postmaster gave him his own bed, and it was decided to send to S— for a doctor the next morning, if the patient did not improve.

Next day the hussar was worse. His batman rode to town on horseback for a doctor. Dunya bound his head in a handkerchief steeped in vinegar and sat by his bed with her sewing. While the postmaster was there, the patient kept groaning and hardly said a word; he did, however, drink down two cups of coffee and, still groaning, ordered himself some dinner. Dunya did not leave him. He was constantly asking for a drink, and Dunya would offer him a tankard of lemonade she had made. The patient kept moistening his lips and each time, as he handed the mug back, he would signal his gratitude by giving young Dunya's hand a feeble squeeze in his own. Towards dinnertime the doctor arrived. He felt the patient's pulse, spoke with him in German, and explained in Russian that he simply needed rest and after a couple of days would be able to take to the road. The hussar handed him twenty-five roubles for the visit and invited him to dinner; the doctor accepted, and they both ate a hearty meal, emptied a bottle of wine and parted on excellent terms.

Another day passed, and the hussar completely recovered. He was exceptionally cheerful and joked unceasingly, now with Dunya, now with the postmaster. He kept whistling tunes, chatting with travellers and registering their road passes in the post book; and he so endeared himself to the good postmaster that by the third morning the postmaster was sorry to part with his charming guest. The day was Sunday; Dunya was getting ready for Mass. The hussar's sleigh was brought up. He took leave of the postmaster, recompensing him generously for board and lodging; he took leave of Dunya too and offered to give her a lift to the church, which lay on the edge of the village. Dunya stood there in two minds…

"What are you afraid of?" her father said to her. "His Honour's not a wolf and won't eat you: take a ride to the church."

Dunya sat herself in the sleigh next to the hussar, the manservant jumped up beside the coachman, the coachman gave a whistle, and the horses galloped off.

The poor postmaster never understood how he, of all people, could have let his Dunya ride with the hussar, how he could have been so blind, what could have possessed his mind at that moment. Not half an hour had passed before his heart started to ache and ache, and anxiety got so much the better of him that he could stand it no longer and went off to Mass himself. As he approached the church, he saw people already dispersing, but there was no Dunya, either in the churchyard or on the porch. He hurriedly entered the church; the priest was coming out of the sanctuary; the sexton was putting out the candles; two old women were still praying in a corner; but there was no Dunya in the church. The poor father forced himself to ask the sexton whether she had been at Mass. The sexton replied that she had not. The postmaster returned home neither dead nor alive. He had one hope left: Dunya, with youthful impulsiveness, might have taken it into her head to ride on to the next post station, where her godmother lived. In an agony of dread he waited for the return of the troika in which he had seen her off. The coachman did not return. Finally, towards evening, he did drive up, alone and drunk, with the deadly news: "Dunya went on past the other station with the hussar."

The blow was more than the old man could bear. He lay down straight away on the same bed where the young trickster had lain the night before. Now, as he reviewed all the circumstances, the postmaster began to realize that the illness was bogus. The poor man fell ill with a violent fever; he was taken to S— and a temporary replacement was appointed. The same doctor that had come to see the hussar treated him too. He confirmed to the postmaster that the young man had been perfectly well: he had even begun to suspect his evil purpose at the time, but had kept quiet for fear of the man's whip. Whether the German was telling the truth or just wanted to make a show of his perspicacity, he certainly did nothing to reassure his poor patient. Hardly had the postmaster recovered from his illness when he applied to the head postmaster in S— for two months' leave of absence; and without saying a word to anyone of his intention, he set off on foot to find his daughter.

From the road pass he knew that Cavalry Captain Minsky was travelling from Smolénsk to St Petersburg. The coachman who was driving him had testified that Dunya cried the whole journey, though she was apparently going of her own free will.

"Perhaps," thought the postmaster, "I'll bring home my little lost sheep."

With this in mind he reached St Petersburg, put up in the house of a retired corporal, his old comrade-in-arms, by the Izmáylovsky barracks, and commenced his quest. He soon learnt that Captain Minsky was in St Petersburg, staying at the Demut Inn.* The postmaster decided to call on him.

Early in the morning he walked into Minsky's ante-room and requested that His Honour be informed that an elderly soldier was asking to meet him. The batman, who was cleaning a boot on a boot tree, made it known that the master was asleep and that he received no one before eleven o'clock. The postmaster went off and returned at the stated time. Minsky came out to him in person in a dressing gown and red skullcap.

"What do you want, my fellow?" he asked him.

The old man's heart overflowed, tears filled his eyes and all he could utter in a quavering voice was: "Your Honour!… In God's name, have the goodness…" Minsky eyed him quickly, flushed, took him by the arm, led him into his sitting room and shut the door after them.

"Your Honour," the old man continued, "what's dropped from the wagon is lost for good. But at least give me back my poor

Dunya. You've taken your pleasure from her, that's for sure. Don't ruin her to no purpose."

"What's done you can never undo," said the young man in extreme confusion. "I've wronged you, and I'm glad to ask your pardon, but don't imagine I could give Dunya up; she'll be happy, I give you my word of honour. What would you do with her? She loves me; she's grown out of her old way of life. Neither of you, neither you nor she, can shut your minds to what's taken place."

Then, poking something under the old man's cuff, he opened the door, and the postmaster, without remembering how, found himself in the street.

For a long time he stood motionless. At length he noticed a roll of paper under his cuff. He pulled it out and unfolded several crumpled five- and ten-rouble banknotes.* Tears once more welled up in his eyes, tears of anger! He squeezed the notes into a little ball and threw them on the ground, stamped his heel on them and left... After walking several paces he stopped, thought for a moment... and returned... but the notes were no longer there. A well-dressed young man, seeing him, ran up to a cabbie, got in hurriedly and shouted, "Away!" The postmaster did not give chase. He resolved to set off home for his post station, but first he wanted to see his poor Dunya just one more time. For this purpose he returned a couple of days later to Minsky's; but the batman told him roughly that the master was receiving no one, pushed him by the chest out of the ante-room and slammed the door in his face. The postmaster stood there, stood there – then left.

That very evening he was walking along Litéynaya Street,* having attended a service at the Church of the Holy Mother of All the Afflicted. Suddenly there dashed by in front of him a smart open carriage, and the postmaster recognized Minsky. The carriage stopped by a three-storeyed house, at the very entrance, and the hussar raced up the steps. A happy thought flashed through the postmaster's mind. He turned back and, coming level with the driver, asked him, "Friend, whose horse is that? Isn't it Minsky's?"

"It certainly is," replied the driver. "But why do you ask?"

"Well, it's like this: your master ordered me to take a note to his Dunya, but it's slipped my mind where this Dunya of his lives."

"Well, just here, on the second floor. You're a bit late with your note, friend. He's already with her himself."

"No matter," rejoined the postmaster with an inexpressible quickening of his heart. "Thanks for the warning, but I'll finish off my task." And with those words he climbed the steps.

The doors were locked. He rang, then waited several agonizing seconds. A key grated; someone opened up.

"Is Avdótya Simeónovna* staying here?" he asked.

"Yes, here," replied a young maidservant. "What do you want her for?"

The postmaster, without replying, stepped into the hall.

"No, no, you mustn't!" the servant shouted after him. "Avdótya Simeónovna's got visitors."

But the postmaster did not listen and strode on. The first two rooms were dark; in the third there was a light. He approached the open door and halted. In the splendidly decorated room Minsky was sitting deep in thought. Dunya, sumptuously dressed in the latest fashion, was sitting on the arm of his chair, like an Englishwoman riding sidesaddle. She was gazing affectionately at Minsky and curling his long black hair on her shimmering fingers. Poor postmaster! Never had his daughter appeared to him so beautiful; he watched her in involuntary admiration. "Who's there?" she asked without looking up. He remained silent. Not hearing an answer, Dunya raised her head... and with a scream fell down on the carpet. Minsky, alarmed, rushed to pick her up; then, suddenly noticing the old postmaster in the doorway, he left Dunya and strode up to him, trembling with anger.

"What do you want?" he said to him through clenched teeth. "Why do you creep after me everywhere like a brigand? Or do you mean to cut my throat? Get out!" And seizing the old man firmly by the collar, he thrust him out onto the steps.

The old man walked back to his lodging. His friend advised him to file a complaint; but the postmaster thought for a moment, then waved his arm and decided to give up. Two days later he set off from St Petersburg back to his post station and resumed his duties.

"It's over two years now that I've lived without Dunya," he concluded, "and there's been neither word nor wraith of her. Whether she's alive or dead, God knows. Anything could be happening. She's not the first or the last that some good-for-nothing traveller has lured away, then kept awhile and thrown over. There's many of them in Petersburg, stupid young things, in satin and velvet today, and tomorrow, you'll see, they'll be sweeping the street with drunks from the taverns. When you think sometimes that Dunya may be coming to grief there too, you can't help – sinful it is, I know – wishing her in the grave..."

That was the story told me by my friend the old postmaster – a story more than once interrupted by tears, which he picturesquely wiped away on the flap of his coat, like the devoted Teréntyich in Dmítriev's brilliant ballad.* These tears were partly induced by the punch, of which he downed five glasses in the course of his narration; nevertheless, they touched my heart deeply. After parting from him, for a long time I couldn't forget the old postmaster, for a long time I kept thinking of poor Dunya*...

Quite recently, as I was riding through the small town of ——, I remembered my friend; I learnt that the post station he had run was now closed down. When I asked, "Is the old postmaster still alive?" no one could give me a satisfactory answer. I decided to visit the area I had known; I took some free horses and set off for the village of N—.

This took place in autumn. Greyish clouds covered the sky; a cold wind blew off the fields of stubble, snatching leaves of red and yellow from trees in its path. I reached the village at sunset and stopped at the little post house. Into the porch (where poor Dunya had once kissed me) there emerged a stout peasant woman, who in answer to my questions said that the old postmaster had died about a year ago; a brewer had moved into the house, and she was the brewer's wife. I began to regret my useless journey and the seven roubles I had spent for nothing.

"What did he die of?" I asked the brewer's wife.

"Drink, sir," she replied.

"And where's he buried?"

"T'other side o' the common, beside his dead missus."

"Someone couldn't take me to his grave, could they?"

"Why not. Oy, Vanka! Enough o' your playing around with the cat. Will you take the gentleman to the cemetery and show him the postmaster's grave?"

At these words an urchin with red hair and one eye ran out to me and led me off across the common.

"Did you know the man that died?" I asked him on the way.

"Course I did. 'E taught me 'ow to cut reed pipes. Sometimes (God rest 'is soul!) 'e'd come out the tavern, and we'd be after 'im shouting 'Grandpa, grandpa! Nuts!' – and he'd give us nuts. 'E was always good to us, 'e was."

"And travellers, do they remember him?"

"There's few passing through now'days. P'raps th' inspector might turn up, but he don't have nowt to do with the dead. Summertime, there were a lady drove by; and, yes, she were asking after the old postmaster and wanting to go to 'is grave."

"What sort of lady?" I asked with curiosity.

"Fine lady she were," answered the young boy. "She were riding in a carriage with six 'orses, with three little posh kids and a nurse and a black pug dog; and when they said to 'er that the old postmaster'd died, she started crying straight away and said to the little 'uns, 'Sit here quietly while I go to the cemetery.' And I were offering to show 'er the way, but the lady said, 'I know the way myself.' And she gave me a five-copeck piece, silver one – such a kind lady!"

We had arrived at the cemetery, a desolate, unfenced place, planted with wooden crosses, but with no stick of a tree for shelter. Never in my life had I seen such a dismal cemetery.

"'Ere's the old postmaster's grave," the boy said to me, jumping onto a heap of sand, into which had been dug a black cross mounted with a copper icon.

"And did the lady come here?" I asked.

"Yes, she did," Vanka answered. "I were watching 'er from a distance. She laid 'erself down 'ere, and were lying a long time. But then the lady walked off to the village; she sent for the priest, gave 'im money and drove away; and me she gave five copecks in silver – nice lady!"

I too gave the young lad a little five-copeck piece; and no longer did I regret either the trip or the seven roubles it cost me.

Young Miss Peasant*

You're lovely, Dúshenka,
whatever clothes you wear.
– Bogdanóvich*

I N ONE OF OUR MORE DISTANT PROVINCES there lay the
property of Iván Petróvich Bérestov. In his youth he had served
in the guards; he took retirement at the beginning of 1797,* withdrew to his country seat, and from then on did no more travelling.
He married a woman of small means but good family, who died
in childbirth when he was off on a hunting trip. The management
of his estate soon brought him consolation. He built a house to
his own design, established a cloth factory, tripled his income and
began to regard himself as the cleverest chap in all the district – an
opinion unchallenged by his neighbours when they drove up for
visits with their families and hounds. On weekdays he used to go
about in a velveteen jacket; on Sundays and holidays he wore a
full coat of home-produced cloth. He kept his accounts himself,
and read nothing but the *Senate Gazette*.* In general people liked
him, though considering him aloof.

It was only his closest neighbour Múromsky who did not get on
with him. A true Russian squire was this one: having squandered
the greater part of his resources in Moscow, he had departed, a

widower now, for his last-remaining estate, where he continued his spendthrift existence, but in a new way. He laid out a park in the English style, spending on it almost all the money he had left. His stable lads were dressed like English jockeys. His daughter had an English governess. His fields were farmed in the English manner.

But Russian grain grows not by foreign means* –

and despite a drastic reduction in outgoings his funds did not increase; even in the country he found ways of contracting new debts.* For all that, he was not thought a stupid man, for he was the first landowner of his province to have the idea of mortgaging his estate to the Trustee Board,* a transaction regarded at that time as extraordinarily complex and venturesome. Of those who criticized him it was Bérestov who voiced the harshest views. Hatred of innovations was a defining feature of his character. He could not speak in measured terms of his neighbour's Anglomania and found constant opportunities to run him down. If he was showing his domains off to a visitor, he would respond to their praise of his estate management by saying with a sly grimace: "Yes, sir! I've a different approach from Grigóry Ivánovich yonder. Why ruin ourselves by copying the English, when the Russian way at least keeps us fed?" These and similar jibes, duly enlarged and elaborated, were zealously brought to Grigóry Ivánovich's attention by the neighbours. The Anglomaniac was as intolerant of criticism as our reviewers. He flew into a rage and called his detractor a bear and a provincial.

Such were the relations between these two landowners when Bérestov's son arrived at the estate for a visit. He had been educated at —— University and was intending to enter military service, but the father would not agree. For a civil-service career the young man felt himself quite unsuited. Neither would give way, and young Alexéi began for the present to live as a country gentleman, growing a moustache for any eventuality.*

Alexéi was in reality a fine fellow. It would certainly have been a shame for his handsome figure never to be shown off in a trim military uniform and, instead of cutting a dash on horseback, for him to spend his youth hunched over official documents. When the neighbours saw him out hunting, always galloping off in front without keeping to the path, they used to say with one accord that he would never make a prudent head of department. Young ladies used to make eyes at him (sometimes could not take their eyes off him!), but Alexéi showed scant interest in them, and they ascribed his indifference to an amorous liaison. In fact a copy of an address from one of his letters was passing from hand to hand:

*To Akulína Petróvna Kúrochkina, Moscow, opposite the Alexéyevsky monastery, at the house of Savélyev the copper-smith, you are most humbly requested to forward this letter to A.N.R.**

Those of my readers who have not lived in the country cannot imagine what a delight these provincial young misses are! Brought up in the open air, in the shade of their garden apple trees, they gather their knowledge of society and life from novelettes.* At an early age solitude, freedom and reading develop in them feelings and emotions unknown to our empty-headed paragons of beauty. For the country miss the jingle of horse bells is itself an adventure; a trip to a nearby town counts as a turning point in history; and a visitor's arrival leaves a long, sometimes lifelong memory. Anyone, of course, may laugh at certain of their oddities; but the mirth of a superficial observer cannot negate their real merits, chief among them distinctiveness of character, or *individualité*, without which, according to Jean Paul, there is no human greatness.* In St Petersburg and Moscow women receive, maybe, a better education, but social convention quickly rubs character smooth and makes personalities as monotonous as their hairdos. Let this not be said in judgement or condemnation; even so, *nota nostra manet*,* as one ancient commentator writes.

It is easy to imagine the impression Alexéi was bound to produce among these young ladies of ours. He was the first man they had met to seem gloomy and disillusioned, the first to speak to them of wasted joys and of his blighted youth. What is more, he wore a black ring bearing the image of a death's head. All this was utterly new in that province. The young ladies were in ecstasies over him.

But the one most fixated by him was my Anglomaniac's daughter Liza (or Betsy, as Grigóry Ivánovich usually called her). The fathers never exchanged visits, and she had not yet seen Alexéi, at a time when all her young neighbours were talking of nothing else. She was seventeen. Black eyes enlivened her dark and very attractive countenance. She was an only child, and so over-indulged. Her high spirits and constant pranks delighted her father and were the despair of her governess Miss Jackson, a prim forty-year-old spinster, who whitened her face and blackened her eyebrows, reread *Pamela** twice a year, received two thousand roubles in remuneration and was dying of boredom in this "barbaric Russia".

Liza's attendant was Nastya; she was a little older, but just as flighty as her mistress. Liza was very fond of her, told her her secrets and made her an accomplice in her schemes; in short, Nastya was a much more important personage on the Prilúchino estate than any confidante in a French tragedy.

"May I go visiting today?" Nastya said one day as she was dressing her mistress.

"By all means. Where to, though?"

"Tugílovo, to the Bérestovs'. It's the cook's wife's name day, and she came over yesterday to ask us to dinner."

"Well, well!" said Liza. "The squires are feuding, but the servants ask each other out!"

"Why should we bother with the squires?" retorted Nastya. "In any case, I belong to you, not to your papa. And you've no quarrel yet with Bérestov Junior. Leave it to the old men to fight, if that makes them happy."

"Nastya, try and get a sight of Alexéi Bérestov, and give me a full account of how he looks and what sort of man he is."

Nastya gave her promise, and the whole day Liza waited impatiently for her return. Nastya appeared in the evening. "Well, Lizavéta Grigóryevna," she said as she came into the room, "I've seen young Bérestov, had a good look at him; we were together the whole day."

"How come? Tell me, tell me from start to finish."

"Very well, miss. We set off – me, and Anísya Yegórovna, Neníla, Dunka—"

"Fine, I know. But what next?"

"With your leave, miss, I'll tell from start to finish. So we arrived just before the dinner. The room was full of people. There were folk from Kólbino, Zakháryevo, the estate manager's wife and daughters, people from Khlúpino—"

"Yes, but Bérestov?"

"Just wait, miss. So we sat down at table, the manager's wife in the place of honour, me next to her... the daughters pulled a face, but I don't care a fig for them—"

"Oh, Nastya, how trying you are with your endless details!"

"And how impatient you are! Well, then we all got up from the table... we'd been sitting there three hours, and the dinner was fantastic; the dessert was blancmange, blue and red and striped... Anyhow we got up from the table and went into the garden to play tag,* and that's when the young squire appeared."

"Well, what about him? Is it true he's so good-looking?"

"Unbelievably good-looking, a stunner, one might say. Tall, slim, cheeks full of colour…"

"Really? But I was so sure he had a pale complexion. Well, then – what sort of man did he seem to you? Gloomy, pensive?"

"What do you mean? Such a crazy chap I've never seen in all my life. He took it into his head to race round at tag with us."

"Race round at tag with you lot? Not possible!"

"Very possible! And what else did he take it into his head to do! When he catches, he kisses!"

"I don't believe it, Nastya – you're fibbing."

"Please yourself; but I'm not fibbing. I'd trouble getting away from him. The whole day he spent with us like that."

"Then how do they say that he's in love and doesn't look at anyone?"

"Don't know, miss, but he was looking at me more than enough, and at Tanya, the manager's daughter too; and at Pasha from Kólbino; and, truth to tell, he didn't turn his nose up at anyone – such a rascal!"

"Amazing! And what's the talk of him at the house?"

"First-rate master, they say: so kind, so cheerful. One thing's not so good: he's too fond of running after the girls. But seems to me that's not a problem either: he'll settle down in time."

"How I'd like to see him!" said Liza with a sigh.

"And what's the problem with that? Tugílovo's not far from us, just three kilometres. Go for a walk that way, or take a ride on horseback; you're sure to meet him. Early every morning the man goes off shooting."

"No, no, that would never do. He might think I'm chasing him. In any case our fathers are feuding, so *I'll* never be allowed to make friends with him... Ah, Nastya! You know what? I'll dress up as a peasant girl!"

"Yes, do that! Put on a thick linen blouse and a sarafan,* and step out boldly for Tugílovo: Bérestov'll spot you, I'll warrant."

"And I can speak the local dialect ever so well. Ah, Nastya, dear Nastya! What a marvellous idea!"

And Liza went to bed firmly resolved to carry out her jolly scheme. The very next day she set about its implementation. She sent to market for coarse linen, blue nankeen and brass buttons; with Nastya's help she cut herself out a blouse and sarafan, got the whole maids' room sewing, and by evening everything was ready. Liza tried the new clothes on and, standing by the mirror, declared she had never seen herself looking so pretty. She rehearsed her part, bowed low as she walked and then wagged her head several times like those pottery cats, spoke with a peasant brogue, giggled behind her sleeve – and won Nastya's wholehearted approval. One thing caused her difficulty: when she tried walking outdoors barefoot, the turf pricked her delicate feet, and the sand and gravel she found unbearable. Nastya helped her out here too: she took a measurement of Liza's foot, ran off to the pasture to find Trofím the shepherd, and ordered from him a pair of tree-bark shoes to fit. The next day Liza woke before dawn. The whole house was still asleep. Nastya waited for the shepherd outside the gates. A horn sounded, and the estate's herd trailed past the manor courtyard. As Trofím passed Nastya, he handed her the little mottled shoes and received a half-rouble from her in reward. Liza quietly got dressed as a peasant girl, whispered instructions to Nastya regarding Miss Jackson, went out by the back steps and ran through the kitchen garden to the open fields.

Dawn was glowing in the east, and golden banks of cloud seemed to be awaiting the sun, like courtiers awaiting their monarch; the bright sky, the morning freshness, the dew, the breeze and the birdsong filled Liza's heart with a childish exuberance; fearful of encountering anyone she knew, she seemed to fly more than walk. As she neared the wood that lay on the edge of her father's property, Liza went more cautiously. It was here that she was to wait for Alexéi. Her heart was pounding unaccountably; but the trepidation that accompanies our juvenile pranks is what constitutes their main appeal. Liza entered the darkness of the wood. The trees' soft, sporadic rustling made her welcome. Her exuberance subsided. Little by little she gave herself up to a pleasant reverie. She was thinking... but can one accurately describe the thoughts of a young lady of seventeen, alone in a wood before six on a spring morning? So there she was, walking deep in thought along a path shadowed on both sides by tall trees, when suddenly a magnificent gun dog started barking at her. Liza was terrified and cried out. At the same time a voice called: "*Tout beau, Sbogar, ici*"*... and a young huntsman appeared from behind some bushes. "Don't be scared, my dear," he said to Liza, "my dog doesn't bite."

Liza had already managed to get over her fright and knew immediately how to make the most of the situation. "Well, no, sir," she said, pretending to be half-frightened, half-shy, "I *am* scared. She's such a fierce dog – look! She'll be jumping up again."

Alexéi – the reader has already recognized him – was meanwhile looking intently at the peasant girl. "I'll see you along, if you're afraid," he said to her. "Will you let me walk beside you?"

"Who's to stop you?" answered Liza. "Feel free: the path's for everyone."

"Where are you from?"

"From Prilúchino; I'm Vasíly the blacksmith's girl; I'm coming for mushrooms." (Liza was carrying a small basket on a cord.) "But you, sir? From Tugílovo, aren't you?"

"Quite so," answered Alexéi. "I'm the young squire's valet."

Alexéi meant to put their relationship on an equal level. But Liza gave him a look and burst out laughing.

"But you're kidding," she said. "It's no scatterbrain you've chanced on. You're the squire hisself, I can see."

"What makes you think that?"

"Everything."

"But what?..."

"How can you not tell master from servant? The dress ain't the same; you talk different; you don't use our lingo to call the dog."

Alexéi was liking Liza more all the time. Being used to familiarity with pretty village girls, he was on the point of putting his arms round her, but Liza dodged away from him and abruptly assumed such a stern and cold expression that, although it made Alexéi laugh, it nonetheless discouraged him from further advances.

"If you want us to go on being friends," she said severely, "then please don't forget yourself."

"Who taught you to be so ultra-cautious?" asked Alexéi with an explosion of laughter. "It wasn't my friend little Nástenka, was it, your mistress's maid? Such are the paths by which civilization spreads!"

Liza felt that she had nearly overstepped her role and immediately corrected herself. "What be you thinking?" she said. "That I ain't never been around in the squire's quarters? Don't you fear: I've heard it all and seen it all. Now though," she went on, "chattering with you, there'll be no mushroom-picking. Off with you, sir, one way, and I'll go t'other. Let's say goodbye…"

Liza wanted to move off. Alexéi held her back by the hand. "What's your name, my darling?"

"Akulína," Liza replied, trying to disengage her fingers from Alexéi's hand. "But let me go, sir; it's time I were off home."

"Well, friend Akulína, I'll be paying a visit, for sure, to your dad Vasíly the blacksmith."

"What?" protested Liza vigorously. "For Christ's sake, don't come! Should they find out at home that I've been chattering in the wood alone with a squire, I'll be in trouble. My father Vasíly the blacksmith'll thrash me to death."

"But I definitely want to meet up with you again."

"Well, some day I'll be coming here again for mushrooms."

"But when?"

"Tomorrow maybe."

"Darling Akulína, I'd give you some kisses, if I dared. So tomorrow, at this time, all right?"

"Yes, yes."

"And you won't let me down?"

"I won't let you down."

"Swear."

"By St Pyátnitsa,* then, I'll be there."

The two youngsters parted. Liza came out of the wood, crossed the pasture, crept into the garden and made a dash for the "farm" building, where Nastya was waiting for her. There she changed, while distractedly answering her impatient accomplice's questions, then made her appearance in the drawing room. The table was laid, breakfast was ready and Miss Jackson, whitened already and corseted into a wineglass shape, was cutting delicate slices of bread. Her father commended her for her early walk. "There's nothing healthier," he said, "than to be up with the dawn."

At this point he adduced several examples of human longevity culled from English magazines, remarking that all those people living to more than a hundred had drunk no spirits and had risen at dawn winter and summer. Liza was not listening to him. She was going over in her mind all the circumstances of the morning's encounter, all of Akulína's conversation with the young huntsman, and her conscience was beginning to prick her. It was no good her protesting to herself that their chat had not exceeded the bounds of propriety and that this joke of hers could not lead to any consequences; her conscience muttered louder than her reason. The promise she had given for the following day worried her more than anything: she came close to deciding firmly against honouring her solemn oath, but Alexéi, after waiting for her in vain, might come to the village in search of Vasíly the blacksmith's daughter, the real Akulína – a fat, pockmarked girl – and so might realize the frivolous prank she had played. This thought appalled Liza, and she decided to turn up in the wood again as Akulína the next morning.

Alexéi, for his part, was in raptures and spent the whole day musing over his new acquaintance. At night a vision of the lovely dark girl assailed his imagination even in sleep. Dawn was scarcely breaking before he was already dressed. Without taking time to load his gun, he went out into the fields with his trusty Sbogar and raced to the promised rendezvous. About half an hour passed in unbearable suspense; then at last he saw the flicker of a blue sarafan among the bushes and rushed to meet his dear Akulína. She greeted his ecstatic gratitude with a smile, but Alexéi immediately observed traces of sadness and anxiety in her face. He wanted to know the cause. Liza confessed that she now viewed her behaviour as frivolous and regretted it: this time she had not wanted to break her pledge, but the present meeting would now be the last, and she begged him to break off the acquaintance, which could lead to no good. All this, it will be understood, was spoken in a peasant dialect, but Alexéi was surprised at thoughts and sentiments uncharacteristic of an unsophisticated girl. He deployed all his eloquence to deflect Akulína from her intention, assured her of the innocence of his desires, promised never to give her reason for remorse but to follow her wishes in everything, and adjured her not to rob him of his one joy – meeting her alone, if only every other day, if only twice a week. He spoke in a language of genuine passion and was at that moment truly in love. Liza listened to him in silence.

"Give me your word," she said finally, "that you'll never seek me out in the village or ask after me. Give me your word not to look for other meetings with me except those that I'll fix myself."

Alexéi was about to swear to her by St Pyátnitsa, but she stopped him with a smile.

"I don't need oaths," Liza said. "Just your promise is enough."

After that they talked as friends, walking together through the wood, until Liza said to him: "It's time."

They parted, and Alexéi, left alone, could not understand how a simple young country girl could have gained such real ascendancy over him in two meetings. His relations with Akulína had the charm of novelty for him, and though the strange peasant girl's stipulations struck him as onerous, the idea of not keeping his word did not even enter his head. The truth was that Alexéi, despite his macabre ring, his mysterious correspondence and his air of gloomy disillusion, was a generous and spontaneous chap with an unspoilt heart susceptible to innocent pleasures.

If I were attending only to my own wishes, then I would certainly go on* to describe in every detail the youngsters' meetings, their burgeoning mutual affection and trust, their occupations, their conversations; but I know that the majority of my readers would not share my enthusiasm. In general such details are bound to seem contrived, so I shall omit them, after saying in brief that not two months had passed before my Alexéi was already head-over-heels in love, and Liza was just as committed, if less demonstrative than he. Both were happy in the present and thought little of the future.

The thought of unbreakable ties quite often crossed their minds; but they never discussed this. Clearly, Alexéi, devoted as he might be to his dear Akulína, remained conscious of the distance that existed between him and the poor peasant girl; and Liza, aware of the enduring animosity between their fathers, dared not hope for a mutual reconciliation. Besides, her vanity was secretly tickled by the dim, romantic hope of finally seeing the young squire of Tugílovo at the feet of the Prilúchino blacksmith's daughter. Suddenly a major event opened the prospect of a change in their relationship.

On one of those bright, cold mornings that enrich our Russian autumns, Iván Petróvich Bérestov went out for a ride on horseback, taking with him, on the off-chance, three pairs of hounds, a groom, and several stable lads with rattles. At the same time Grigóry Ivánovich Múromsky, enticed by the fine weather, had his dock-tailed mare saddled and rode off for a trot round his Anglicized domains. As he approached the wood, he saw his neighbour sitting proudly aloft in a Cossack caftan lined with fox fur and on the lookout for a hare that the lads were flushing out of the bushes with shouts and rattles. Had Grigóry Ivánovich been able to foresee this encounter, he would of course have turned aside; but he came across Bérestov quite unexpectedly and found himself suddenly only a pistol shot away. There was nothing to be done: Múromsky, the cultured European, rode up to his antagonist and greeted him politely. Bérestov replied with the sort of cordiality with which a chained bear would greet members of the public when commanded by his trainer. At that moment the hare leapt out of the wood and ran off across the open grassland. Bérestov and the groom hallooed at the top of their voices, unleashed the dogs and galloped off in hot pursuit. Múromsky's horse, never having been hunting, took fright and bolted. Múromsky, who boasted of his fine horsemanship, gave the mare full rein and was inwardly glad at the opportune escape from his unfriendly interlocutor. But the horse, galloping up to a gully it had not noticed, suddenly shied and threw Múromsky. He fell quite heavily on the frozen earth and lay there cursing his dock-tailed mare, which, as though coming to its senses, stopped on the spot as soon as it felt itself riderless. Iván Petróvich galloped over to him and enquired whether he was injured. Meanwhile the groom brought up the guilty mare, holding it by the bridle. He helped Múromsky hoist himself into the saddle, and Bérestov invited him to his house. Múromsky, considering himself under an obligation, could not refuse; and in this way Bérestov returned home in triumph, having caught the hare and leading his enemy wounded and like a prisoner of war.

Over breakfast the neighbours started chatting in a friendly enough way. Múromsky asked Bérestov for a carriage, acknowledging that because of his injury he was not in a state to ride home on horseback. Bérestov saw him all the way to the steps, but Múromsky would not leave till he had extracted his word of honour that he would come to Prilúchino the very next day, along with Alexéi Ivánovich, for a friendly dinner. In such a way an ancient and deep-rooted enmity seemed ready to come to an end, thanks to the skittishness of a dock-tailed mare.

Liza ran out to meet Grigóry Ivánovich. What's the reason for this, Papa?" she said with surprise. "Why are you limping? Where's your horse? Whose carriage is this?"

"You'll never guess, *my dear*,"* replied Grigóry Ivánovich, and he related to her all that had happened. Liza could not believe her ears. Grigóry Ivánovich, without letting her recover herself, explained that the next day both Bérestovs would be with him for dinner.

"What are you saying?" said Liza, turning pale. "The Bérestovs, father and son! Dining with us tomorrow! No, Papa: as you please, but I shall not appear."

"What's all this? Are you out of your mind?" the father protested. "Why this new-found shyness? Or are you cherishing an ancestral hatred for them, like some romantic heroine? That's enough. Don't play the fool."

"No, Papa, not for anything in the world, not for treasures of any sort, will I show myself in front of the Bérestovs."

Grigóry Ivánovich shrugged his shoulders and argued with her no more, for he knew that no one would ever get anything out of her by contradicting her; and he withdrew to have a rest after his memorable outing.

Liza Grigóryevna went off to her room and summoned Nastya. They had a long discussion about the next day's visit. What would Alexéi think if he recognized his Akulína in the well-educated young lady of the manor? What opinion would he have of her conduct and principles, and of her judgement? On the other hand Liza very much wanted to see what the effect of such an unexpected encounter would have on him... Suddenly an idea occurred to her. She immediately shared it with Nastya. Both of them welcomed it as a brainwave and decided to put it into effect come what may.

The next day at breakfast Grigóry Ivánovich asked his daughter whether she still intended to hide from the Bérestovs.

"Papa," replied Liza, "I will receive them, if that's your wish, but on one condition: whatever I look like in front of them, whatever I do, you won't tell me off and you won't show any sign of surprise or displeasure."

"Up to your pranks again!" said Grigóry Ivánovich with a laugh. "All right, all right, I agree, do as you want, you little black-eyed jester." With those words he kissed her on the forehead, and Liza ran off to get ready.

At exactly two o'clock a carriage of local build, harnessed with six horses, drove into the courtyard and trundled round the circle of rich green lawn. Old Bérestov climbed the front steps with the help of two of Múromsky's liveried footmen. His son arrived behind him on horseback, and together they entered the dining room, where the table was already laid. Múromsky received his neighbours with all possible attention, offered them a tour of the park and menagerie before dinner, and conducted them along paths meticulously swept and gravelled. Old Bérestov inwardly regretted the work and time wasted on such pointless fads, but kept silent out of politeness. His son shared neither the thrifty landowner's disapproval nor the vain Anglomaniac's enthusiasm; he was waiting impatiently for the appearance of the host's daughter, about whom he had heard much; and though his heart (as we know) was already engaged, any attractive young woman always had free entry to his imagination.

On entering the drawing room they sat down as a threesome: the old men recalled former times and anecdotes of their army days, while Alexéi wondered what role he should play in Liza's presence. He decided that a cold detachment would best suit any eventuality and prepared himself accordingly. The door opened; he turned his head with such indifference, such lofty unconcern, that the heart of the most inveterate flirt must surely have faltered. Unfortunately, instead of Liza, there entered the elderly Miss Jackson, whitened, corseted, with lowered eyes and a perfunctory curtsey; and Alexéi's brilliant defensive manoeuvre was completely thwarted. He had not managed to remarshal his forces when the door opened again, and this time Liza entered. All rose; the father was about to begin introducing the visitors when he suddenly paused and hastily bit his lip... Liza, his dusky Liza, was whitened to the ears, her eyebrows blackened more than Miss Jackson's; false curls, much fairer than her own hair, were fluffed up like a Louis XIV *perruque*; absurdly full sleeves stuck out like one of Madame de Pompadour's hooped skirts;* her waist was laced tight like a letter X; and all her mother's jewels not yet pawned were glittering on her fingers, neck and ears. Alexéi failed to recognize his Akulína in this ludicrous and flamboyant young miss. His father approached and kissed her hand, and he followed on with distaste. As he touched her dainty white fingers, they seemed to him to be trembling. In the process he managed to catch sight of a foot, deliberately exposed to view, and shod as provocatively as possible. This reconciled him a little to the rest of her attire. As for the white paint and black make-up, truth to tell, in the simplicity of his heart he had not noticed them at first glance and even later remained unaware of them. Grigóry Ivánovich, mindful of his promise, tried not to show any sign of surprise; but his daughter's prank seemed to him so funny that he could hardly contain himself. The prim Englishwoman was in no mood for laughter. She suspected that the black and white make-up had been purloined from her dressing table, and a crimson flush of annoyance showed through the simulated pallor of her face. She cast blistering glances at the young prankster, who, deferring all explanations till later, pretended not to notice.

They sat down at table. Alexéi went on acting the part of someone preoccupied and abstracted. Liza played coy and spoke through her teeth in a sing-song voice, exclusively in French. Her father kept glancing at her all the time, not comprehending her purpose but finding the whole performance extremely amusing. The Englishwoman fumed in silence. Only Iván Petróvich seemed at home, ate enough for two, drank his full share and laughed at his own jokes, chattering and chortling in an ever more amicable fashion.

At length they rose from the table; the guests departed, and Grigóry Ivánovich gave vent to his laughter and questions.

"What put it into your head to play the fool with them?" he asked Liza. "And do you know what? That white paint really suited you; I never go into the mysteries of female toilette, but if I were you, I'd start using white paint; not too much of course, just a little."

Liza was in raptures over the success of her stratagem. She gave her father a hug, promised to give thought to his advice, and ran off to pacify the enraged Miss Jackson, who could hardly be prevailed upon to unlock her door and listen to Liza's excuses: she'd been embarrassed to appear so dark-complexioned before men she didn't know, she hadn't dared to request... she was sure that the good, kind Miss Jackson would forgive her... etc., etc. Miss

Jackson, satisfied that Liza was not meaning to make fun of her, calmed down, gave Liza a kiss and, as a token of reconciliation, presented her with a pot of English whitener, which Liza accepted with a profession of sincere gratitude.

The reader will have guessed that the next morning Liza lost no time in appearing at their rendezvous in the wood.

"You was at our gentry's house last night, sir?" she said immediately to Alexéi. "What did you think of the young mistress?"

Alexéi replied that he had not taken any notice of her.

"Pity," Liza retorted.

"Why so?" asked Alexéi.

"It's that I'd like to've asked you whether it's true what they say…"

"What do they say?" asked Alexéi.

"Is it true what they say, that I look like the young mistress?"

"What rubbish! Next to you she's a monster of monsters."

"Ah, sir, that's a wicked thing to say. Our young mistress is so white-skinned, so up with the fashions! How could I be at all like her?"

Alexéi swore to her that she was better-looking than any white-faced young lady in the world and, to reassure her completely, began to describe her mistress in such comical terms that Liza laughed her heart out.

"All the same," she said with a sigh, "though maybe the young mistress is funny, next to her I'm still a dunce that can't read or write."

"No-oo!" said Alexéi. "What a thing to be upset about! But if you want, I'll teach you to read and write straight away."

"All right, then," said Liza. "Why not give it a try?"

"For sure, my dear; let's begin right now."

They sat down. Alexéi took a pencil and notebook out of his pocket, and it was amazing how quickly Akulína learnt the alphabet. Alexéi could not get over his surprise at her intelligence. The following morning she wanted to have a go at writing. At first the pencil would not do what she wanted, but after several minutes she was beginning to draw letters quite decently.

"Astounding!" Alexéi kept saying. "We're learning better than by Lancaster's system."*

In fact, by the third lesson Akulína was already spelling out *Natálya the Boyar's Daughter*,* interspersing the reading with comments that truly astonished Alexéi, and covering a whole sheet with scribbled aphorisms culled from the same story.

A week passed, and a correspondence started between them. A post office was set up in the hollow of an old oak tree. Nastya secretly carried out the duties of postman. There Alexéi brought letters written in a bold hand, and there he found on plain blue paper the scrawl of his beloved. Akulína was manifestly developing a better style of expression, and her mind was growing markedly more mature and cultivated.

Meanwhile the new acquaintance between Iván Petróvich Bérestov and Grigóry Ivánovich Múromsky was growing closer and closer, and it soon developed into friendship, in the following manner. It often occurred to Múromsky that on Iván Petróvich's death the whole of his property would pass into the hands of

Alexéi Ivánovich; that in such an eventuality Alexéi Ivánovich would be one of the richest landowners in the province; and that there was no reason at all for him not to get married to Liza. Old Bérestov, for his part, while recognizing in his neighbour a certain eccentricity (or, in his own phraseology, an "English folly"), could not deny that he had many outstanding merits: a singular ingenuity, for example; also Grigóry Ivánovich was a close relative of Count Pronsky, a distinguished and influential man; the Count might be useful to Alexéi, and Múromsky (so Iván Petróvich thought) would doubtless be delighted at the chance of marrying off his daughter advantageously. The old men had been pondering all this independently, until finally they discussed it together, embraced, undertook to arrange the matter as best they could, and set about organizing it each from his own side.

Múromsky faced a difficulty: that of persuading his Betsy to strike up a closer acquaintance with Alexéi, whom she had not set eyes on since that memorable dinner. Indeed, they had not seemed to like each other much; Alexéi, at least, had never returned to Prilúchino; and Liza had gone off to her room every time Iván Petróvich had favoured them with a visit. "But," thought Grigóry Ivánovich, "if I were to have Alexéi with me every day, then Betsy would be sure to fall in love with him. That's in the nature of things. Time will take care of everything."

Iván Petróvich was less concerned for the success of his plans. That same evening he summoned his son into his office, lit his pipe, and after a short silence said: "Alyósha, why is it that you haven't mentioned a military career for so long? Or are you no longer attracted by a hussar's uniform?"

"No, father," replied Alexéi respectfully, "I can see that it's not to your liking that I should join the hussars. It's my duty to follow your wishes."

"Fine," replied Iván Petróvich, "I can see that you're an obedient son. That reassures me. It's certainly not my wish to force you into anything. I don't insist upon your entering... for the moment... the civil service; but in the meantime I mean to get you married."

"Married to whom, father?" asked Alexéi in surprise.

"To Lizavéta Grigóryevna Múromskaya," replied Iván Petróvich. "An excellent match, eh?"

"Father, I'm not giving any thought to marriage yet."

"You're not giving it thought, so I've been giving it thought for you – and I've thought it through."

"With respect, father, Liza Múromskaya doesn't appeal to me in the least."

"She will appeal to you. 'Live together, love together.'"

"I don't think I'm the sort to make her happy."

"Her happiness isn't your problem. Well, then? Is this how you respect your father's wishes? A fine thing!"

"Make of it what you will, but I don't want to marry, and I won't marry."

"You *will* marry, or you can go to damnation. And the property, as God is holy – I'll sell it and spend it, and I'll not leave you a mite. I give you three days for reflection, and in the meantime don't you dare show yourself to me."

Alexéi knew that once his father had taken something into his head, then (to use Tarás Skotínin's expression*) even with a nail you'd never knock it out of him. But Alexéi was like his father, and it was just as hard to talk him round. He went off to his room and began to reflect on the limits of parental authority, on Lizavéta Grigóryevna, on his father's solemn vow to reduce him to penury, and finally on Akulína. And for the first time he saw clearly that he was wildly in love with her; the romantic idea of marrying a peasant girl and living by his own exertions came into his head, and the more he thought about this drastic step, the more sense he made of it. For some time now the woodland trysts had been interrupted by rainy weather. He wrote a letter to Akulína in the boldest handwriting and the most impassioned style, explained to her the impending catastrophe, and went straight on to offer her his hand. He took the letter immediately to the postbox in the hollow tree and went to bed well pleased with himself.

Early the next morning Alexéi, firm in his intention, drove to Múromsky's to give him a frank account of himself. He hoped to arouse his sympathy and win him to his side.

"Is Grigóry Ivánovich at home?" he asked as he reined his horse in at the porch of the Prilúchino mansion.

"Afraid not, sir," a servant replied. "Grigóry Ivánovich has been pleased to ride out for the morning."

"How annoying!" thought Alexéi. "Is Lizavéta Grigóryevna at home, at least?"

"She is at home, sir."

Alexéi leapt from his horse, handed the reins to the footman and went off, not waiting to be announced.

"It's all going to be settled," he thought as he approached the drawing room. "I'll have it out with her in person."

He went in... and stood transfixed! Liza... no, Akulína, dear dusky Akulína – not in a sarafan, but in a white morning dress – was sitting by a window reading his letter. She was so engrossed that she did not hear him enter. Alexéi could not restrain a delighted exclamation. Liza started, raised her head, cried out and tried to run away. He rushed to hold her back.

"Akulína, Akulína..."

Liza tried to free herself from him... "*Mais laissez-moi donc, monsieur; mais êtes-vous fou?*"* she kept repeating, as she turned away.

"Akulína, my darling Akulína..." he kept saying, kissing her hands.

Miss Jackson, who witnessed the scene, knew not what to make of it. At that moment the door opened and in came Grigóry Ivánovich.

"Aha!" said Múromsky. "So you've evidently got it all settled..."

Readers will spare me the superfluous task of describing the denouement.

A History of
Goryúkhino Village

A History of Goryúkhino Village

S HOULD GOD SEND ME READERS, it may interest them to learn how it was that I decided to write *A History of Goryúkhino Village*. For that I need to go into some preliminary details.

Goryúkhino village was where I was born, of honourable and noble parents, on 1st April 1801;* and I received my basic education from our parish clerk. It was to this esteemed personage that I owe the enthusiasm I developed later for reading and for literary endeavours in general. My progress, though slow, was solid, for nearly all that I knew by the age of ten has stayed on till now in my memory – a memory poor by nature, which I was not allowed to overburden as my health was equally poor.

For me a literary vocation has always seemed one most to be desired. My parents, respectable but unsophisticated folk brought up in the old way, never did any reading, and there was never a book in the whole house, beyond an ABC purchased for me, some yearbooks and *The Modern Primer*.* Reading the *Primer* was for long my favourite occupation. I knew it by heart, but even so I discovered in it each day new, unsuspected delights. Second to General Plemyánnikov* (whom Father had once served as adjutant), Kurgánov seemed to me the greatest of men. I used to question everyone about him, and to my regret no one could satisfy my curiosity: no one had known him personally, and the only answer I got to all my enquiries was that Kurgánov was author of *The Modern Primer*, which I knew perfectly well already. Like some ancient demigod, he was wrapped in a cloud of obscurity; sometimes I even doubted the fact of his existence. I came to think of his name as a fiction and the reports of him as empty myth* awaiting the researches of a new Niebuhr.* He continued, however, to haunt my imagination. I tried to endow this mysterious figure with a visual image of some kind and eventually decided that he must have looked like the district court assessor Koryuchkin, a little old man with red nose and twinkling eyes.

In 1812 I was taken to Moscow and enrolled in Karl Ivánovich Meyer's boarding school – where I spent no more than three months, as we were sent away in advance of the enemy occupation. I returned to the country. After the expulsion of the Twelve Nations,* they wanted to take me back to Moscow to see if Karl Ivánovich had returned to his old heap of ashes or, if not, to enrol me in another college; but Mother yielded to my entreaties that I be left in the country, since my health prevented me from getting up from bed at seven o'clock as all boarding schools normally required. In this way I reached the age of sixteen, without progressing beyond my basic education but playing bat-and-ball with my chums, the only skill in which I had gained reasonable proficiency during my stay at boarding school.

It was at this time that I enlisted as a cadet in the —— infantry regiment, in which I remained till last year, 18—. My life in the regiment has left me with few pleasant memories beyond my promotion to officer and winnings of 245 roubles at a time when I had only one rouble sixty left in my pocket. The deaths of my beloved parents obliged me to hand in my resignation and travel here to my ancestral estate.

This milestone in my life is so important to me that I propose to enlarge upon it, after begging my benevolent readers' pardon if I abuse their patient attention.

It was an overcast day in autumn. When I reached the post station where I had to turn off for Goryúkhino, I hired some free horses and travelled on by the country road. I am of a naturally quiet disposition, but I was so overwhelmed with impatience to see once more the places where I had spent my best years that I repeatedly urged my coachman forward, now promising him money for a drink, now threatening him with a beating; and as it was easier for me to strike him on the back than to dig my purse out and undo it, I confess that I actually hit him two or three times – something I had never done in my life, as for some unknown reason I have a soft spot for the coach-driver fraternity. The coachman drove his team of three on, but I had the impression that, in coachman fashion, while audibly egging the horses on and brandishing his whip, he nonetheless kept reining them in. Finally I caught a distant sight of the Goryúkhino wood, and ten minutes later I entered the manor courtyard. My heart pounded as I looked around me with indescribable emotion. I had not seen Goryúkhino for eight years. The birch saplings that had been planted by the fence within my lifetime had grown up and were now tall, well-branched trees. The courtyard, once adorned with three straight flower beds on either side of a broad gravelled drive, had now reverted to an unmown field in which a cow was grazing. My light carriage drew up by the front steps. My manservant went off to open the doors, but they were nailed up, even though there were shutters open and the house seemed occupied. A peasant woman emerged from the servants' outbuilding and asked who I wanted. When she learnt that the master had arrived, she ran off to the building again, and I was soon surrounded by the house serfs. I was touched to the depths of my heart to see familiar and unfamiliar faces – and to exchange friendly embraces with them all: my boyhood playmates were now grown farmhands, and the little girls who had once sat about on the floor waiting for errands were now married wenches. Men were weeping. To the women I kept saying cheekily: "You're not so young any more!" – and they would answer me with animation: "You're not so good-looking any more either, sir!" I was taken round to the back porch: my nurse came out to meet me and hugged me with tears and sobs as if I were a much enduring Odysseus.* Some ran off to heat up the bathhouse. The cook, who with no duties to perform had grown himself a beard, offered to prepare me dinner – or supper, since it was already getting dark. They immediately cleared out the rooms for me where my nurse had been living with my late mother's maids. So I found myself in my humble ancestral home and went to sleep in the same room where I had been born twenty-three years before.

I spent the next three weeks busy with all kinds of chores – I was engaged with court assessors, marshals of nobility and every imaginable government official. I finally received title to my inheritance and was invested with ownership of my patrimonial lands.* I started to relax; but soon the tedium of inactivity began to torment me. I had not yet made the acquaintance of my kindly and estimable neighbour ——. I was a complete stranger to estate management. What my nurse had to say – I had promoted her to housekeeper and administrator – consisted of just fifteen household anecdotes, which were of the greatest interest to me, but which she always related in the same way, so that she became for me a second *Modern Primer*, where I knew on which page to find every little line. The good old *Primer* itself I discovered in a storeroom, among all kinds of bric-a-brac, in a pitiful state. I brought it out into the light and started perusing it; but for me Kurgánov had lost his old appeal: I read him through once more and never opened him again.

In this impasse an idea came to me: why not try writing something myself? The indulgent reader already knows that my early education was sadly deficient and that I never had the opportunity to catch up on what I had missed, fooling around as I did to the age of sixteen with the kids on the estate, and from then on marching from province to province, from billet to billet, consorting with

Jews and food-sellers, gaming on tattered billiard tables and stomping through mud.

What is more, being a writer seemed to me so problematic, so unattainable for uninitiated folk like me, that the thought of taking up a pen frightened me at first. Dared I hope ever to join the community of authors, when my burning desire to meet with a single one had never been realized? But this reminds me of an incident that I want to relate to demonstrate my undying passion for our native literature.

In 1820, when still a cadet, I happened to be on official duty in St Petersburg. I was in the city for a week and, despite not having a single acquaintance there, I had an extremely jolly time: every day I would slip off quietly to the theatre, to the fourth-level gallery. I got to know all the actors by name and fell madly in love with the girl who one Sunday was playing Amalia with great skill in *Misanthropy and Remorse.** Each morning, on my way back from headquarters, I was in the habit of calling in at a cheap little café where I would read the literary reviews over a cup of chocolate. On one occasion I was sitting engrossed in a critical article in the *Well-Intentioned.** Someone in a pea-green overcoat approached me and gently pulled out from under my magazine a copy of the *Hamburg Gazette.** I was so absorbed that I did not raise my eyes. The stranger ordered himself a beef steak and sat down opposite me. I kept reading, without paying him attention. He meanwhile ate his breakfast, angrily upbraided the waiter for poor service, drank down a half-bottle of wine and left. Two young chaps were breakfasting in the same place. "Do you know who that was?" one asked the other. "That's B—, the writer."*

"Writer!" I exclaimed involuntarily – then, leaving my journal half-read and my drink half-drunk, I rushed off to pay and, without waiting for the change, ran out into the street. Looking in all directions, I caught sight of the pea-green coat in the distance and set off after it along the Nevsky Prospékt almost at a run. After I had gone a few steps I suddenly felt myself being pulled to a halt. I looked round and a guards officer warned me not to "push him off the pavement, but halt and stand to attention". After this reprimand I was more careful. Frustratingly, I kept meeting officers and halting, while the writer was all the time moving off ahead of me. In all my life I had never found my soldier's greatcoat such a nuisance, and in all my life I had never felt so jealous of epaulettes. At length I only caught up with the pea-green coat at the Aníchkov Bridge.

"Excuse me for asking," I said, raising my hand to my brow, "are you Mr B—, whose excellent articles I have had the pleasure of reading in *The Champion of Enlightenment*?"*

"Certainly not, sir," he replied, "I'm not a writer but a man of the law. I know —— very well, though; a quarter of an hour ago I met him at the Politséysky Bridge."*

In this way my esteem for Russian literature cost me thirty copecks in lost change, an officer's reprimand and almost an arrest – all for nothing.

Despite every dictate of my reason, I could not rid my head of the foolhardy idea of becoming a writer. At length, being no longer in a state to resist my native impulse, I sewed myself together a thick exercise book with the firm intention of filling it with something or other. All types of poetry (I had not yet given thought to humble prose) I analysed and evaluated, and I set my mind firmly on an epic poem, drawn from the history of our fatherland. It did not take me long to find a hero. I chose Ryúrik* – and set to work.

I had gained some facility for verse by transcribing notebooks that were doing the rounds of our officers, namely: *A Dangerous Neighbour,** *Critique of a Moscow Boulevard*, *To the Présnensky Ponds** and others. Even so my epic moved slowly, and I gave it up at the third line. I concluded that the epic genre was not for me, and I began a Ryúrik tragedy. The tragedy did not get going. I tried to turn it into a ballad – but somehow I could not manage the ballad either. Finally inspiration dawned on me, and I began, and successfully completed, a caption to a portrait of Ryúrik.

Even though my caption was not entirely unworthy of attention, particularly as a young versifier's first composition, I nonetheless came to the view that I was not born to be a poet, and I rested content with this first effort. But my creative endeavours had so wed me to literary pursuits that I was unable to part with notebook and inkwell: I would lower myself to prose writing. Initially, not wishing to be bothered with preliminary research, drawing up a plan, linking up sections and so on, I conceived the idea of writing down separate, unconnected, unordered thoughts in whatever guise they presented themselves to me. Unfortunately thoughts would not come to mind, and for two whole days all that occurred to me was the following observation:

> The one who flouts reason's laws and habitually follows the promptings of emotion often goes astray and exposes himself to belated remorse.

The thought is of course true, but far from original. So, setting thoughts aside, I applied myself to stories; but lacking the ability, through inexperience, to organize a fictional plot, I chose notable anecdotes that I had heard at some time or another from various people and endeavoured to embellish the truth with lively narration and sometimes too with my own imaginative colouring. In putting these stories together I gradually refined my style and learnt to express myself accurately, attractively and fluently. But my material quickly ran out, and I began to search anew for a subject for my literary activity.

The idea of abandoning second-hand and untrustworthy anecdotes for the recital of great events that really happened had long stirred my imagination. To be observer, judge and prophet of epochs and nations seemed to me the highest rank a writer could attain. But what history could I, with my pitiable education, write which men of great learning and good judgement had not tackled before me? What historical subjects had they not already exhausted? Should I begin to write a universal history – as if the immortal achievement of Abbé Millot* did not already exist?

Should I turn to the history of the fatherland? What can I say after Tatíshchev, Boltín and Gólikov?* And am I one to dig around in chronicles and decipher the hidden meaning of an obsolete language, when I have never managed to master Old Slavonic numerals?* I contemplated a history of more limited scope, such as a history of our provincial capital… but even here so many obstacles, to me insurmountable! – a journey to the city, visits to the governor and the bishop, requests for access to archives and monastery storerooms, and so on. A history of our district town I would have found easier, but it would neither interest the philosopher nor the man of affairs and would offer little raw material for eloquence: — was only named a town in 17—, and the one significant event recorded in its archives is the terrible fire that took place ten years ago and destroyed the market and government offices.

An unexpected occurrence resolved my uncertainties. A laundry woman hanging linen up in the attic found an old basket full of wood chips, rubbish and books. The whole house knew of my fondness for reading. While I was sitting at my notebook chewing a pen and contemplating an attempt at some rustic homilies, my housekeeper dragged the basket triumphantly into my room, exclaiming gleefully: "Books! Books!"

"Books!" I repeated eagerly and rushed to the basket. There I beheld a whole heap of books bound in green and blue paper. It was a collection of old yearbooks. This realization cooled my enthusiasm, but even so I was pleased at the unexpected discovery;

they were books, after all, and I generously rewarded the washer-woman's initiative with half a rouble in silver.* Left alone, I began to look through my yearbooks, which soon gripped my attention. They constituted an unbroken series from 1744 to 1799 – that is, exactly fifty-five years.* The sheets of blue paper regularly bound within yearbooks were all covered in old-fashioned handwriting. As I cast an eye over these lines, I saw with surprise that they included not only household accounts and notes about the weather, but also snippets of historical information concerning Goryúkhino village. I quickly undertook an analysis of these precious records and soon discovered that they presented a complete history of my ancestral estate over nearly a full century, in the strictest chrono-logical order. On top of that they contained an inexhaustible fund of economic, statistical, meteorological and other scientific data. From then on the study of these records occupied me exclusively, since I realized the possibility of extracting from them a narrative that would be well ordered, interesting and instructive. Once I had familiarized myself enough with this precious archive, I began to look for new sources on the history of Goryúkhino village, and I was soon astonished by the abundance of them. Having devoted six whole months to preliminary research, I finally embarked on the task I had so long looked forward to, and with God's help I completed it on the 3rd of this month, November 1827. Now, like a certain fellow historian whose name I cannot remember, having come to the end of my arduous enterprise, I lay down my pen and walk with sorrow into my garden to reflect on what I have achieved.* It seems to me too, now that I have written the History of Goryúkhino, that the world no longer needs me: my duty is fulfilled, and it is time for me to take my rest.

———————

I append here a list of the sources that I have used in compiling the History of Goryúkhino:

1. A collection of old yearbooks. Fifty-four issues. The first twenty issues are full of old-fashioned handwriting with diacritical marks for abbreviations and figures.* This chronicle was composed by my great-grandfather Andréi Stepánovich Belkin. It is notable for the clarity and concision of its style, for example: "*4th May*. Snow. Trishka beaten for rudeness. *6th*. Brown cow died. Senka beaten for drunkenness. *8th*. Bright weather. *9th*. Rain and snow. Trishka beaten due to weather. *11th*. Bright weather. Fresh snow. Caught 3 hares..." – and so on, without any discussion... The remaining thirty-five issues are written in different hands, for the most part in the so-called "shopkeeper's" hand, with and without diacritical marks, generally in a prolix and disjointed style, without regard to correct spelling. In some places a woman's hand is observable. In this batch come the entries made by my grandfather Iván Andréyevich Belkin and my grandmother (his wife) Yevpráxiya Alexéyevna, also those of the estate manager Garbovítsky.

2. A chronicle by the Goryúkhino parish clerk. This interesting manuscript I discovered at the house of my parish priest, who is married to the chronicler's daughter. The opening pages had been torn out and used by the priest's children as paper darts. One of these landed in the middle of my yard. I picked it up and was about to return it to the children when I noticed that it was covered in writing. I saw from the first lines that the dart was made from a chronicle and by good fortune managed to salvage the remainder. This chronicle, acquired by me in exchange for 300 litres of oats, is remarkable for its profundity of thought and its exceptional grandiloquence.

3. Oral traditions. I have not overlooked any sources of information. But I am particularly indebted to Agraféna Trífonova, mother of village elder Avdéi, the mistress (or ex-mistress, so it is said) of the manager Garbovítsky.

4. Poll-tax registers (and income and expenditure ledgers) with notes by previous village elders regarding the morals and condition of the peasants.

———————

The territory that bears the name of its capital Goryúkhino covers an area of more than 1,600 hectares of the earth's surface. Its population amounts to sixty-three souls. To the north it borders on the estates of Deriúkhovo and Perkúkhovo, the inhabitants of which are poverty-stricken, emaciated and small in stature, while their lordly proprietors spend their time on the warlike practice of hare-coursing. To the south the River Sivka separates it from the domains of the free arable farmers of Karachevo, turbulent neighbours known for the violence and ferocity of their ways. To the west it is enclosed by the rich pastures of Zakháryino that thrive under the sway of wise and enlightened landowners. To the east it adjoins wild, unpeopled lands and an impenetrable marsh where nothing grows but cranberries, where the only sound is the monotonous croaking of frogs, and which an old superstition holds to be a demon's abode.

NB: Its name is actually Demon's Marsh. The story is told that a half-witted herdswoman used to tend a herd of pigs not far from this lonely spot. She became pregnant and was quite unable satisfactorily to account for her condition. Popular rumour blamed the marsh demon; but this tale is beneath a historian's attention, and after Niebuhr it would be inexcusable to credit it.

———————————

From ancient times Goryúkhino has been famed for its fruitfulness and its propitious climate. Rye, oats, barley and buckwheat grow in its fertile meadows. A birch copse and a forest of firs provide the inhabitants with timber and firewood for building and heating dwellings. There is no shortage of hazelnuts, cranberries, cowberries and bilberries. Mushrooms grow in unusual quantities; when fried in sour cream they make a delicious, if unhealthy dish. The pond is full of carp, and in the River Sivka there are plenty of pike and burbot.

———————————

The inhabitants of Goyrúkhino are for the most part of middling height and of strong and vigorous constitution; their eyes are grey; their hair is blond or ginger.* The women are distinctive for their snub noses, high cheekbones and stoutness. (NB: "Buxom wench": this expression occurs frequently in the village elder's notes to the poll-tax registers.) The men are decent and industrious (especially on their own allotments); they are fearless and combative; many of them go after bears single-handed and are famous in the locality as fist-fighters; in general they are all susceptible to the physical pleasure of drunkenness. The women, on top of their domestic tasks, share a large part of the men's work; and they are not behind the menfolk in boldness: few of them stand in awe of the village elder. They organize a formidable community patrol, staying awake to keep watch over the manor house, and they are called "*kopéyshchitsi*" (from the Slavic word *kopyó* for "spear"). The main duty of the *kopéyshchitsi* is to bang a stone as fast as possible on an iron plate, and thereby deter any criminal enterprise. They are as chaste as they are good-looking, and they respond to any attempted liberties sternly and forthrightly.

The people of Goryúkhino have for a long time done a big trade in baskets, shoes and other articles made from tree bark. This is facilitated by the River Sivka, across which they paddle canoes in spring, like the Scandinavians of old, and which at other seasons they cross on foot, rolling their breeches up to the knee beforehand.

The Goryúkhino dialect is definitely a branch of Slavonic, but differs from it as much as Russian does. It is full of contractions and elisions; some letters are completely unsounded or are replaced by different ones. Even so, it is easy for a Great-Russian* to understand someone from Goryúkhino, and vice versa.

The men normally used to get married in their thirteenth year to twenty-year-old girls. The wives used to beat their husbands for four or five years, then the husbands began to beat their wives. In this way both sexes had their period of dominance, and equilibrium was achieved.

Funeral rites were carried out in the following manner. On the very day of death the deceased was carried off to the cemetery, so that a dead body should not pointlessly occupy spare space in the hut. This led to cases where, to the indescribable joy of relatives, a corpse might sneeze or yawn at the very time when it was being carried out of the village in a coffin. Wives would lament their husbands, wailing and adding the words: "Brave light of my eyes! Who will be with me now you've forsaken me? What do I have to remember you by?" When everyone was back from the cemetery a wake in the deceased's honour would commence, and relatives and friends would get themselves drunk for two or three days or even for a whole week, depending on their enthusiasm and attachment to the deceased's memory. These ancient rites have even been maintained to the present time.

The dress of Goryúkhino men used to consist of a shirt worn over breeches – a distinguishing mark of their Slavonic origin. In winter they used to wear a sheepskin coat, though more for its smart look than for any real need, as the coat was normally slung over one shoulder and thrown off for the least job that required movement.

The sciences, arts and poetry were in quite a flourishing state in the Goryúkhino of old. As well as the priest and church officials there were always plenty of others who could read and write. The chronicles mention a local clerk, Terénty, who lived around 1767 and who could write not only with his right hand but with his left. This remarkable man was renowned in the neighbourhood for his production of letters, petitions, travel authorizations and other certificates. Having been punished repeatedly for his skill and helpfulness and for his role in various important events,* he died at a ripe old age, just as he was training himself to write with his right foot, the script of both his hands being by then too recognizable. He also plays, as the reader will see below, an important role in the history of Goryúkhino.*

Music has always been a favourite art form with cultivated Goryúkhino folk. The balalaika and bagpipes, to the delight of all sensitive hearts, can be heard to this day in their homes and especially in the ancient public edifice decorated with a fir tree and the sign of the two-headed eagle.*

Poetry once flourished in ancient Goryúkhino. The verses of Arkhíp the Bald have been preserved in the memory of later generations up to the present. In delicacy they are a match for the *Eclogues* of the renowned Virgil,* and in richness of imagination they far outstrip the idylls of Mr Sumarókov.* Although they fall short of the latest works of our poets in elegance of style, they equal them in inventiveness and wit. As an example let us quote these satirical lines:

> To the boyar's manor house
> sly Antón, the elder, goes,
> goes to tell him what he owes,
> records, scratched on wood, he shows.
> Puzzled boyar stands there blinking,
> of what's owed he has no inkling.
> O you rascally Antón,
> you've defrauded everyone –
> boyars, serfs face penury,
> while your wife's in luxury!

Now that I have acquainted my reader in this way with the ethnographical and statistical data relating to Goryúkhino and with the manners and customs of its inhabitants, let us proceed to the narrative itself.

Legendary Times

TRIFON THE VILLAGE ELDER

G ORYÚKHINO'S form of government has changed several times. It came in turn under the rule of constables chosen by the community and of estate managers appointed by the landowner, then finally under the direct control of the landowners themselves. I will expand on the advantages and disadvantages of these different modes of government in the course of my narrative.

The establishment and earliest settlement of Goryúkhino are shrouded in a fog of uncertainty. Obscure traditions declare that Goryúkhino was once a rich and extensive village, that its inhabitants were all well off, and that the rent, collected once a year, required several wagons to convey it to its unknown recipient. At that time the buying price of everything was cheap, and the selling price high. Estate managers did not exist; village elders gave offence to no one; the inhabitants worked little, but lived in joy and harmony; and herdsmen tended their flocks in boots. We must not let ourselves be led astray by this beguiling picture. The idea of a golden age is common to all nations; it demonstrates only that people are never satisfied with the present and, having through experience little hope for the future, they use all the colours of their imagination to embellish a past that is beyond recall. What is reliable is the following.

Goryúkhino village has belonged to the illustrious Belkin family from ancient times. But my predecessors, owning as they did numerous other family estates, disregarded this remote region. Goryúkhino's material contribution was small, and it was administered by constables chosen by the so-called Common Council – the people meeting in assembly.

In the course of time, however, the Belkin family domains were broken up and fell into disarray. The impoverished grandchildren of a rich grandfather were unable to drop their extravagant habits and demanded continuance of a full income from lands that were now a tenth of what they had been.* Menacing injunctions kept arriving one after the other. The village elder read them in the assembly; the constables spoke out; the community protested; and, instead of double the rent, the gentry received devious excuses and obsequious complaints written on greasy paper sealed with a two-copeck piece.

A dark storm cloud was hanging over Goryúkhino, but nobody gave it a thought. In the final year of the reign of Trifon, the last popularly elected village elder, on the very day of the patronal festival, when all the people were gathering noisily around the "house of entertainment" (tavern, in plain language) or roaming the streets with their arms round each other, loudly trumpeting the songs of Arkhíp the Bald, there drove into the village a small covered wickerwork carriage drawn by a pair of nags more dead than alive. On the coachbox sat a Jew in rags, and out of the carriage there poked a head in a peaked cap which seemed to be eyeing the merrymakers with curiosity. People greeted the vehicle with hilarity and coarse jibes (NB: "The idiots rolled up the edges of their garments like a tube and jeered at the Jewish driver, yelling facetiously, 'Yid, Yid, munch a pig's ear!...'" – *Chronicle of the Goryúkhino Parish Clerk*). But imagine their surprise when the carriage stopped in the middle of the village and out jumped the newcomer calling in an imperious voice for Trifon the elder. This dignitary proved to be in the "house of entertainment", from which he was brought respectfully by two constables supporting him by the arms. The stranger gave him a fearsome look, handed him a letter and ordered him to read it out forthwith. Goryúkhino elders never used to read anything themselves, and Trifon was illiterate. Avdéi the local clerk was sent for. He was discovered not far away, asleep under a fence in an alleyway, and brought before the stranger. But either because he had been forewarned, or out of sudden panic, or from a premonition of trouble, he saw the words of the letter, though boldly written, swimming before his eyes, and he was unable to make them out. With dreadful imprecations the stranger sent Trifon the elder and Avdéi the clerk away to have a sleep and deferred the reading of the letter to the next day. He then strode off to the estate office, with the Jew carrying his little travelling case after him.

The folk of Goryúkhino had been watching this unprecedented event in mute astonishment, but soon carriage, Jew and stranger were forgotten. The day ended with noise and merriment, and Goryúkhino went to bed with no inkling of what awaited it.

With the rising of the morning sun the inhabitants were awakened by a knock on the window and a summons to a meeting of the Common Council. The citizens turned up one by one in the yard of the estate office, which served as the place of assembly. Their eyes were dim and red, and their faces puffy. Yawning and scratching themselves, they watched as the man in the peaked cap and an old blue caftan stood self-importantly on the office steps, and they tried to recognize his features, which they had seen once before. The elder Trifon and the clerk Avdéi were standing beside him hatless and with a look of subservience and profound misery.

"Are all here?" asked the stranger.

"Everyone here?" repeated the elder.

"Everyone," answered the citizenry.

The elder then announced that a letter had been received from the lord of the manor and instructed the clerk to read it out in the hearing of the community. Avdéi stepped forward and read the following in a thunderous voice:

(A note records: "I copied out this ominous message in the house of Trifon the elder; he had kept it in an icon chest with other mementos of his reign over Goryúkhino." I have not been able to find this interesting letter.)

Trifon Ivánov!

My agent ——, *the bearer of this letter, is travelling to Goryúkhino village, my ancestral property, to take over its management. Forthwith on his arrival you are to call the peasants together and make known to them my will as lord of the manor, namely: they, the peasants, are to attend to my agent* ——*'s instructions as though they were my own. Whatever he demands they are to carry out without question; otherwise he,* ——, *is to deal with them with all possible severity. I have been driven to this by their unconscionable disobedience and, Trifon Ivánov, by your reprehensible connivance.*

Signed: XX

Then ——, standing with legs apart like a letter X and with arms akimbo like a Φ, delivered the following brief and unambiguous speech:

"Watch yourselves with me, you folk. Don't try being too clever. I know you're a pampered lot, but have no fear – I'll knock any fancy ideas out of your heads quicker than you'll lose yesterday's hangover."

There was no hangover left in any head. Thunderstruck, the folk of Goryúkhino lowered their eyes and dispersed to their homes aghast.

The Regime of Estate Manager ——*

—— took up the reins of government and proceeded to set up his own political system, one meriting particular scrutiny.

The system was based primarily on the following principle: the richer a peasant, the more impudent he will be; the poorer a peasant, the more submissive. Accordingly —— aimed for submissiveness throughout the property as the chief peasant virtue. He demanded a list of peasants and sorted them into rich and poor.

1. Arrears of payment were apportioned among the well-to-do peasants and exacted from them with the utmost rigour.
2. Unsatisfactory and work-shy wastrels were promptly set to work growing crops: if he reckoned their work to be inadequate, he put them at other peasants' disposal as labourers, in return for a discretionary payment; those so delivered into serfdom had the full right to redeem themselves by paying, in addition to their arrears, a double rate of poll tax.

All communal obligations fell on the well-to-do peasants. Military conscription was a triumph for this rapacious administrator: all the rich peasants in turn bought themselves out of army service, till finally a useless or destitute one came up for selection.[1] Common councils were abolished. He collected rents in small amounts throughout the year. But he also imposed additional levies without warning. The rents the peasants paid were not so much more than before, but there was no way they could earn or save enough cash. Within three years Goryúkhino was completely impoverished.

Goryúkhino became a wretched place; the market was abandoned; the songs of Arkhíp the Bald were heard no more. Small children went begging. One half of the peasants were put to growing crops; the other half worked as labourers; and the day of the patronal festival became, to use the chronicler's expression, no day of joy and celebration, but an anniversary of sorrow and painful remembrance.

....

---

1 "The damned manager put Antón Timoféyev in irons, but old Timoféi bought his son out for 100 roubles; the manager chained up Petrúshka Yereméyev, and his father bought him out for 68 roubles; the damned fellow wanted to put Lyokha Tarásov in chains, but he escaped into the forest, and the manager was extremely vexed at this and cursed and swore; instead the drunkard Vanka was carted off to town and delivered for conscription." (Complaint lodged by Goryúkhino peasants.)

Notes

p. 1, *The Young Hopeful*: A comedy (*Nédorosl*) of 1782 by the Russian writer Denís Ivánovich Fonvízin (1745–92). The words quoted come from Act IV, Sc. 8. The play is a satire on the philistinism of the Russian gentry, and Pushkin's quotation was intended to convey to his readers an ignorant and rustic background similar to Belkin's. In this scene Prostakóva tries vainly to show off her son Mitrofán's education in front of guests, one of whom suggests that the obviously ignorant lad might nonetheless be competent in history; but the Russian *istóriya*, like the French *histoire*, can mean both "history" and "story", leading Prostakóva and her brother Skotínin to mistake "history" for "his stories". By recalling this joke, Pushkin is not only signalling his own storyteller Belkin's lack of education, but also pointing up the ambiguous nature of the "stories" that follow, which are presented by the fictional and unreliable Belkin as being "in large part true".

p. 3, *without any alteration or comment*: As will be seen from his footnotes, the inconstant "editor" does alter one passage of the letter (by deleting an anecdote) and comments on another.

p. 7, *my own estate being mentioned somewhere*: In *The Blizzard*, on p. 26.

p. 8, *16th November 1830*: Since the writer did not receive the editor's letter of 15th November until the 23rd, this date cannot be correct. For a discussion of this "mistake" see the Extra Material on p. 169.

p. 8, *A.P.*: The first edition of 1831 presented *Belkin's Stories* simply as "edited and published by A.P.", though many would have guessed "A.P." to be Alexander Pushkin. The second edition of 1834 was included in a volume more openly entitled "Stories edited and published by Alexander Pushkin".

p. 9, *The Shot*: The story was dated by Pushkin 12th–14th October (1830), the fourth in order of composition. It was narrated to Belkin by "Lieutenant Colonel I.L.P.", whose encounters with Silvio described in Chapter 1 must be dated to no later than 1820, and whose visit to the Count and Countess in Chapter 2 would have taken place no later than spring 1825.

p. 9, *Baratýnsky*: The poet Yevgény Abrámovich Baratýnsky (1800–44) was a friend and contemporary of Pushkin's. The quotation is from Baratýnsky's narrative poem *The Ball*. In it the hero Arsény tells how he was cheated of his first love by a more personable rival. Arsény, consumed by jealousy, reacts like Silvio in this story: by behaving offensively he provokes a duel with the rival. In the duel Arsény is shot but survives in ongoing bitterness.

p. 9, *An Evening under Canvas*: A short story, published in 1823, by Pushkin's contemporary Alexándr Alexándrovich

Bestúzhev (1797–1837), a popular author of blood-and-thunder melodramas, whom Pushkin is gently parodying in this story. In Bestúzhev's tale, the hero Mechin, outraged by an insult to his fiancée, demands satisfaction and is severely wounded in the ensuing duel. Yet on his recovery he finds himself rejected by the girl in favour of his rich and titled adversary. Although sworn to revenge and still owed his shot in the duel, he is posted to the Danube, where a bullet all but kills him. On his return to Russia his thirst for vengeance is thwarted by the sight of his former fiancée now abandoned by the young rake and dying of consumption – a sentimental ending eschewed by Pushkin. Pushkin refers to the work rather than to the writer, probably because Bestúzhev, as a convicted participant in the Decembrist uprising of 1825, was thereafter regarded with deep disfavour by the authorities in St Petersburg. Unable to publish in his own name, he used the pen name Marlínsky.

p. 15, *Burtsóv... Denís Davýdov celebrated*: General Denís Vasílyevich Davýdov (1784–1839) was a poet and writer on military subjects. As a young officer in the hussars in the early 1800s he began writing poems reflecting army life, including three drinking songs of 1804 that celebrated his comrade and drinking partner Lieutenant Alexándr Petróvich Burtsóv (d.1813). Later, Davýdov was a friend of Pushkin's.

p. 17, *picking ripe cherries from his cap... at me*: An autobiographical touch. While living in Kishinyóv (1820–23), Pushkin had been challenged to a duel by an army officer because of a provocative remark he had made after a game of cards. He turned up for the duel with cherries and ate them while his opponent aimed. The officer shot first and missed; Pushkin departed without firing.

p. 25, *Hetaerists... Alexander Ypsilantis' uprising... the battle of Skulyány*: Alexander Ypsilantis (Alexándr Konstantínovich Ipsilánti, 1792–1828), a general of Greek-Balkan origin in the Russian army, became head of the so-called Philikē Hetaireia ("Society of Friends"), a secret society of those committed to fight for Greek independence from the Turkish Empire. In February 1821, Ypsilantis led a ragtag force of Hetaerists across the River Prut (a tributary of the Danube), from Russian Bessarabia into Turkish Moldavia, and attempted to raise a rebellion against the Turks. The rebellion failed, and on 17th June 1821 the few hundred surviving Hetaerists were annihilated by vastly superior Turkish forces at the battle of Skulyány (Sculeni) on the Prut. Pushkin may be suggesting a parallel between Silvio's superfluous death in the cause of Greek independence at Skulyány and that of Lord Byron three years later in the same cause at Missolonghi.

p. 26, *The Blizzard*: Dated by Pushkin 20th October (1830), last of the stories in order of composition. Belkin ascribes the story to "Miss K.I.T.", who also narrated 'Young Miss Peasant'. The action is set between 1811 and 1815, encompassing Napoleon's invasion of Russia in 1812 and the subsequent Russian triumph over France.

p. 26, *Zhukóvsky*: The epigraph consists of lines from *Svetlána* (1808–12), a melodramatic ballad of the supernatural by Vasíly Andréyevich Zhukóvsky (1783–1852). Svetlána, the eponymous heroine of Zhukóvsky's story, has a nightmare, in which her absent lover comes to her and carries her off in a sleigh across a snowy landscape. They approach a remote church, where Svetlána expects them to get married; but the congregation are awaiting a burial, not a wedding. After racing on in the sleigh through a blizzard Svetlána is abandoned in the snow and undergoes further nightmarish experiences before awakening and being happily reunited with her lover. One target of Pushkin's parody here is a recent vogue for tales of romantic elopements and dead bridegrooms returning from limbo.

p. 26, *Boston... five copecks a time*: Boston was a form of whist, popular in late-eighteenth-century France, the name of which is said to originate from the siege of Boston (1775–76) in the American War of Independence. Play was normally for money, but among families like Márya Gavrílovna's amounts would be trifling.

p. 36, *1812*: The year of Napoleon's invasion of Russia. By late August Napoleon had advanced to within 100 kilometres of Moscow, when the Russian armies tried to block his progress at Borodinó. A ferocious battle took place there on 26th August. Tens of thousands of men were killed or wounded on each side. The battle, however, was indecisive, and the Russian commander-in-chief Kutúzov decided that to preserve

Russian fighting power he must retreat beyond Moscow, which Napoleon reached seven days later. The Russians' refusal to capitulate, their depletion of French resources by scorched-earth tactics and by attacks on Napoleon's overextended supply lines, and the approach of winter, finally compelled Napoleon to abandon Moscow and retreat. During the following two years the Russian armies led by Alexander I, and joined by Prussian and Austrian forces, drove the French armies back through Poland, Germany and France till in 1814 they captured Paris and secured Napoleon's abdication. This was the high point of Alexander's career: he and the Russian troops returned home to popular acclaim.

p. 36, *Artemisia*: Artemisia II was sister and wife of Mausolus, ruler of Caria in Asia Minor. When Mausolus died in *c.*353 BC, Artemisia succeeded him; she erected in their capital Halicarnassus a massive monument to her late husband called thereafter the "Mausoleum", which became one of the seven wonders of the ancient world. Through her devotion to her husband's memory Artemisia came to be regarded as a model of loyal widowhood.

p. 37, *Vive Henri-Quatre*: "Long live Henry IV!" (French), words from the historical comedy *La Partie de chasse de Henri IV* (Act III, Sc. 2) by Charles Collé (1709–83). The work, celebrating the first French king of the Bourbon dynasty (r.1572–1610), became popular again in Paris at the time of the Bourbon restoration in 1814.

p. 37, *Tyrolean waltzes*: Austrian forces had fought with the Russians against Napoleon in the European campaigns of 1813 and 1814.

p. 37, *Joconde*: A comic opera by Nicolò de Malte (Nicolas Isouard, 1773–1818), a Maltese composer of French ancestry, who came to Paris via Italy at the end of the eighteenth century; written in 1814, the opera was a great success at the time when the Russian army was occupying Paris. The opera was staged in St Petersburg the next year.

p. 37, *and in the air they tossed their bonnets*: A quotation from the comedy *Woe from Wit* (Act II, Sc. 5) by Alexándr Sergéyevich Griboyédov (1795–1829):

The women shouted out: Hoorah!
and in the air they tossed their bonnets.

The speaker is ridiculing Russian women for falling for men in uniforms.

p. 38, *Se amor non è, che dunque*: "If love it's not, what else then?" (Italian). The beginning of the first line of the sonnet by Petrarch (1304–74): 'S'amor non è, che dunque è quel ch'io sento?' ('If love it's not, what else then am I feeling?'), no. 132 of the *Rime sparse, in vita di Madonna Laura*.

p. 40, *Saint-Preux's opening letter*: Márya Gavrílovna is thinking of the popular French epistolary novel by Jean-Jacques Rousseau (1712–78), first published in 1761, *Julie, ou la*

Nouvelle Héloïse about a young woman, Julie d'Étange, and her young tutor Saint-Preux. In the first letter of the novel Saint-Preux confesses to Julie his dilemma: he has fallen in love with her, but is convinced that circumstances on both sides must prevent their ever marrying. Is he to yield to his desire to go on seeing and talking to her each day, or is he to master his love and leave the household?

p. 41, *Vilna*: I.e. Vilnius, now capital of Lithuania, but then a city in the Russian Empire not far from the frontier where Napoleon was preparing to invade Russia.

p. 44, *The Undertaker*: Dated by Pushkin 9th September (1830), the earliest of the stories to be written. Belkin ascribed the story to "Manager (*prikáshchik*) B.V." In Pushkin's time *prikáshchik* (or *prikázchik*) usually denoted someone of fairly low rank who managed something for someone else; it was used of the stewards or estate managers who administered the estates of landed proprietors for them; in more urban contexts it was used of domestic stewards (house managers), or of employees in businesses who managed a shop or office on behalf of the proprietor. I have called B.V. a "manager" to embrace all these meanings. We are not told who the "manager B.V." was. The only *prikáshchik* mentioned in the story is the house manager in charge of the widow Tryúkhina's household, who sent someone to tell Prókhorov about the widow's death and with whom he later exchanged "a knowing look" in the deceased's room; perhaps it was this house manager who knew Prókhorov well enough to pick up this story about him. True, the house manager only appears in Prókhorov's dream, but it would be typical of Pushkin's humour to have this "ghost story" narrated by a character from the protagonist's nightmare. The story is set in the year 1817. Pushkin is gently parodying the current vogue for ghost stories.

p. 44, *Derzhávin*: Gavríla Románovich Derzhávin (1743–1816), eminent Russian poet and statesman. These lines are taken from his long ode 'The Waterfall' (1798). In this passage an ageing general sits by a waterfall and muses on the transience of the world's power and glory.

p. 44, *Adrián Prókhorov's*: For the interesting autobiographical references in this story, see the Extra Material on p. 168.

p. 44, *from Basmánnaya to Nikítskaya Street*: Basmánnaya and Nikítskaya Street are on opposite sides of Moscow. Basmánnaya is a district and street to the east, and Nikítskaya Street (leading to the Nikítsky Gate) is to the west. The locations are connected with Pushkin's stay in Moscow in the summer of 1830. Pushkin's uncle Vasíly Lvovich Pushkin lived on Basmánnaya Street and died there on 20th August that year. Pushkin took on the arrangements for his funeral. As mentioned in the Extra Material on p. 168, Pushkin's fiancée Natálya Goncharóva lived on Nikítskaya, and nearby were the premises of a funeral director named Adriyán. Near the Nikítsky Gate stands the Church of the Great Ascension, mentioned later; it was at this church in February 1831, five months after writing the story, that Pushkin married Natálya Goncharóva.

p. 45, *both Shakespeare and Walter Scott… jocular characters*: Shakespeare in *Hamlet* (Act v, Sc. 1); and Sir Walter Scott in *The Bride of Lammermoor* (Chapter 24).

p. 46, *Razgulyáy*: Name of a square and quarter in Basmánnaya district, where Adrián used to live.

p. 46, *three Masonic knocks on the door*: As part of the initiation ceremony for a new member of a Masonic lodge, the candidate's sponsor would knock on the door three times.

p. 47, *Pogorélsky's postman*: A retired postman, Onúfrich, was the hero of a short story 'Lafértovskaya Mákovnitsa' (1825) by Antóny Pogorélsky, pseudonym of Alexéi Alexéyevich Peróvsky (1787–1836), a Hoffmannesque tale of the supernatural. Pushkin admired the story and had given it an enthusiastic review.

p. 47, *with axe, in homespun battledress*: A line from the poem 'Dura Pakhómovna' by Alexándr Yefímovich Izmáylov (1779–1831), describing a watchman called Fadéyich.

p. 48, *unserer Kundleute*: "Of our customers" (German).

p. 49, *his face… bound in red morocco leather*: A simile borrowed from the playwright Yákov Borísovich Knyazhnín (1742–91), in whose comedy *The Braggart* (1786) one character describes another as

with face as bloated as a law book
in red morocco-leather binding.

p. 55, *The Postmaster*: In the Russia of Pushkin's day the government maintained "post stations", furnished with a supply of horses, at intervals of thirty or more kilometres along the principal roads. Each station was managed by an official, the post-station superintendent or "postmaster", part of whose job was to see that government couriers and other government personnel, and (so far as resources allowed) private travellers, were provided with horses to carry them on to the next station. Government couriers had first call on available horses; after them other travellers were allocated horses in order of rank on production of a "road pass", a document certifying their name, rank and route of permitted travel; travellers of low standing might have to wait some time for a horse to become available. At remote post stations facilities for refreshment and accommodation were notoriously sparse. This story was dated by Pushkin 14th September (1830), the second in order of composition. Belkin ascribes it to "Titular Counsellor A.G.N.". "Titular Counsellor" (*titulyárny sovétnik*) was the title of the ninth rank in the imperial civil service, equivalent to an army captain. The story takes place between 1816 and about 1823.

p. 55, *collegiate registrar*: "Collegiate registrar" (*kollézhsky registrátor*) was the fourteenth and lowest rank in the Russian civil service in imperial times. Postmasters, previously unranked, were given this rank in a decree of 1808 in order to protect them from verbal and physical abuse by angry customers.

p. 55, *Prince Vyázemsky*: Pushkin has slightly adapted two lines from the beginning of the poem 'Post Station' (1825) by his friend the writer and critic Prince Pyótr Vyázemsky (1792–1878), in which Vyázemsky reflects on the discomforts and frustrations of travelling on Russian roads. In Vyázemsky's original the whole passage (lines 1–7) reads as follows:

> I hate to hear "*Viator, sta!*" –
> or (rendered in officialese)
> "No horses left. Just wait there please!" –
> when some officious registrar
> (but at the post station a tsar!) –
> with these words – would they'd make him choke! –
> intimidates us travelling folk.

[Line 1: "*Viator, sta!*", Vyázemsky uses this Latin expression, meaning "Stay, traveller!"]

p. 55, *unlamented clerks of old Muscovy... brigands of Murom*: The narrator refers first to the *podyáchiye*, clerks in the old Muscovite administration who had a reputation for dishonesty and intrigue. The forests around Murom, an ancient city east of Moscow on the Oká river, were reputedly infested with brigands.

p. 56, *official of the sixth rank*: A collegiate counsellor (*kollézhsky sovétnik*) in the imperial civil service, equivalent to the military rank of colonel.

p. 57, *passed over... governor's dinner*: It was the tradition at formal dinners, though dying out by Pushkin's time, for guests to be served in order of rank. Pushkin has in mind a personal experience here: when visiting Georgia in 1829, the year before composing this story, he had been invited to dine with the military governor of Tbilisi, General Stepán Stepánovich Strekálov, but because of the rank of the other guests, including some English generals, Pushkin was repeatedly passed over in the serving and left the table hungry (see *Journey to Arzrum* (1835), Chapter 2).

p. 58, *story of the prodigal son*: See Luke 15:11–32 and the Extra Material, pp. 166–67.

p. 59, *glass of punch*: In Russia of this period, punch was a popular drink made from boiling water or tea, vodka or rum, sugar, and sometimes lemon, spices, etc.

p. 59, *from when I've had an interest in such things*: Clearly a quotation, but no source has yet been identified.

p. 60, *Simeón Vyrin*: For the postmaster's Christian name see the second note to p. 67.

p. 65, *Demut Inn*: A fashionable hotel in central St Petersburg, established in the 1760s by Phillip-Jacob Demuth (d.1802) from Strasbourg. Pushkin himself sometimes stayed there.

p. 66, *five- and ten-rouble banknotes*: This is the reading of the original 1831 edition; the 1834 edition, probably in error, reads "fifty-rouble banknotes".

p. 67, *Litéynaya Street*: A street in central St Petersburg, now Litéyny Prospékt.

p. 67, *Avdótya Simeónovna*: To hide his identity, the old post-master refers to his daughter by her name and patronymic, the formal Russian way of referring to people with whom they are not on familiar terms. Avdótya is the full form of the name of which "Dunya" is an affectionate diminutive; and Simeónovna means "daughter of Simeón" (the old man's Christian name). In the first edition of 1831 Dunya is called here and just below "Avdótya Samsónovna" (Avdótya, daughter of Samsón), though earlier her father is named *Simeón* Vyrin. In the errata to the 1831 edition, "Simeón" in the earlier passage is amended to "Samsón", thus achieving consistency in that edition; but in his 1834 edition Pushkin names the father "Simeón" in all three places, and it is this edition I have followed, as representing Pushkin's final decision on the name.

p. 69, *Teréntyich in Dmítriev's brilliant ballad*: Iván Ivánovich Dmítriev (1760–1837) was a popular author of satires, fables and other poetry. His humorous ballad *Karikatúra* (1792) tells the story of a landowner who, returning home after many years of army service, finds his wife gone. His loyal old servant Teréntyich explains that in his absence she kept bad company and harboured criminals in the house, one of whom was caught and betrayed her; she was arrested, taken to the local town and not seen again. "God knows whether she's alive or dead," sobs Teréntyich, using the same homely phrase that Vyrin uses: "neither word nor wraith of her". And he is so upset that he has to stoop down to wipe his tears on the flap of his coat. Thus far there are clear parallels with Dunya's fate, as imagined by her father; but the ballad ends with the landowner getting over the loss of his wife, remarrying and becoming a respected local magistrate.

p. 69, *poor Dunya*: This phrase recalls a popular sentimental story by Pushkin's older contemporary Nikolái Karamzín (1766–1826) entitled *Poor Liza* (1792). In the story Liza, a country girl, comes to Moscow and is befriended and seduced by a young aristocratic soldier, who then throws her over for another woman; Liza subsequently drowns herself in a pond. By putting the phrase "poor Dunya" four times into the mouths of her father and the narrator, Pushkin is encouraging the reader to believe what they believe – that Dunya has met a fate similar to Liza's.

p. 72, *Young Miss Peasant*: Dated by Pushkin 20th September (1830), third in order of composition. Belkin ascribes it to "Miss K.I.T", who also narrated 'The Blizzard'. The story is set around 1816–18.

p. 72, *Bogdanóvich*: Ippolít Fyódorovich Bogdanóvich (1743–1803) was a writer of witty and lightly erotic verse, whose work had a strong influence on the young Pushkin. The quotation is from Book 2 of his most important and popular composition, the narrative poem *Dúshenka* (1783).

p. 72, *took retirement at the beginning of 1797*: On succeeding his mother Catherine II in 1796 the Emperor Paul (r.1796–1801) started reorganizing the Russian army and sent into retirement a number of officers, especially in the guards, who had served in the previous reign.

p. 72, *Senate Gazette*: The *Senate Gazette* was a weekly publication, founded in 1808, which set out new government dispositions.

p. 73, *But Russian grain grows not by foreign means*: A line, slightly modified, from the satire *Molière, Your Gift's Unique, Incomparable!...* (1808) by the prolific dramatist and impresario Prince Alexándr Alexándrovich Shakhovskóy (1777–1846).

p. 73, *contracting new debts*: Múromsky's extravagance in aping foreign ways seems to be based on the behaviour of a member of Pushkin's own prospective family. His fiancée Natálya's paternal grandfather Afanásy Nikoláyevich Goncharóv (c.1760–1832) "showed himself... adept at spending money... When he died in 1832 he left debts of half a million roubles. He enlarged [his mansion] and filled it with French furniture and Venetian glass; extended the park, adding bowers, grottoes and classical statues at every turn of the walks; built orangeries and pineries; and set up a stud farm, constructing an immense manège for the training and exhibition of his thoroughbreds..." (T.J. Binyon, *Pushkin: A Biography* p. 289)

p. 73, *Trustee Board*: The Trustee Board (*Opekúnsky Sovét*) was an organization set up under Catherine the Great to safeguard the interests of noble widows, children and orphans; the Board was also empowered to advance money to noblemen against mortgages on their estates. Pushkin had personal experience of their workings: not only was a large part of his father's estates mortgaged with the Board, but on his arrival at Bóldino Pushkin was trying to mortgage his own estate of Kistenevo with them.

p. 74, *growing a moustache for any eventuality*: If Alexéi were to join a regiment of hussars, to wear a moustache would be compulsory.

p. 74, *To Akulína... A.N.R*: The significance of these names to the rest of the story is enigmatic. Could the envelope actually have been a prop in Alexéi's role play as a mystery man with other love interests, designed to intrigue the daughters of the local gentry while at the same time keeping them at arms' length? Ironically, Alexéi was later to believe himself in love with Akulína, a blacksmith's daughter, who could be said to have "forwarded" his affection to a different persona.

p. 75, *in the shade of their garden apple trees... from novelettes:* In the Garden of Eden innocent Eve, under the legendary apple tree, had eaten the fruit that had given her the perilous knowledge of good and evil; here Pushkin is suggesting that innocent young Russian ladies brought up in the country gain their perilous knowledge of the world by devouring romantic novels.

p. 75, *individualité... human greatness*: Jean Paul was the pen name of a prolific German Romantic writer, popular in his day, Johann Paul Friedrich Richter (1763–1825). The reference here is to a French compilation of his thoughts,

Pensées de Jean Paul extraites de tous ses ouvrages (Paris, 1829), where the relevant passage reads as follows: "*Respectez l'individualité dans l'homme; elle est la racine de tout ce qu'il a de bien.*"

p. 75, *nota nostra manet*: "Our comment stands" (Latin). No one has identified the "ancient commentator" said to be the source of this expression.

p. 76, *Pamela*: The epistolary novel *Pamela, or Virtue Rewarded* (1740), by the English writer Samuel Richardson (1689–1761). The first part of the book deals with the attempted seduction of an innocent servant girl by a young aristocrat, who ends up by marrying her. The book had been very popular throughout Europe, but was by now somewhat passé.

p. 77, *play tag*: In Russian "play *gorélki*". A popular game: as B.O. Unbegaun explains, "the players, in couples, place themselves one behind the other, all except one, who stands at the front of the line. Then the last couple at the end of the line separate and start running forward, each on a different side, and try to join up in front without being caught by the other player, who tries to prevent them from doing so."

p. 79, *sarafan*: A sarafan was a full-length sleeveless dress often worn by peasant women over a long-sleeved blouse.

p. 80, *Tout beau, Sbogar, ici*: "Steady, Sbogar, come here" (French). It is tempting to identify the dog's breed as Dalmatian, named as it is after a young Dalmatian brigand Jean Sbogar, hero of a popular French novel, *Jean Sbogar* (1818), by Charles

Nodier (1780–1844). Though not regular hunting dogs, Dalmatians have sometimes been used as such.

p. 83, *St Pyátnitsa*: *Pyátnitsa* is the Russian for Friday, in Greek *paraskeví*. Hence the Greek Christian third-century virgin martyr St Paraskevi was popularly known in Russia as St Paraskéva-Pyátnitsa or St Pyátnitsa. In Russia St (Paraskéva-) Pyátnitsa was revered as the patron saint of marriage, so her invocation here by Akulína is pointed.

p. 86, *If I were... I would certainly go on*: Interestingly, the two verbs here are grammatically masculine, not feminine, in the Russian, indicating that the voice here is not Miss K.I.T.'s, but that of Belkin or "A.P." as editor.

p. 88, *my dear*: Múromsky speaks these two words in English.

p. 91, *Madame de Pompadour's hooped skirts*: Madame de Pompadour (1721–64) was from 1745 till her death mistress of King Louis XV (r.1715–74) and a leading influence at the French court, in fashion and much else.

p. 94, *Lancaster's system*: A method of reciprocal teaching, designed to promote mass education, in which the more advanced pupils aided the rest; the method, promoted by the Englishman Joseph Lancaster (1778–1838), was fashionable in Russia at the beginning of the nineteenth century. Aitken and Budgen point out that before the Decembrist uprising the method had been used by liberal officers in some army regiments in order to spread ideas of reform to the lower ranks.

p. 94, *Natálya the Boyar's Daughter*: A tale (1792) of innocent love
by Nikolái Karamzín (1766–1826) concerning a hero (another
Alexéi) prevented by parental opposition from marrying a heroine who is illiterate; the story ends happily with their marriage.
The "aphorisms" in Karamzín's tale are almost all about love.

p. 97, *Tarás Skotínin's expression*: Tarás Skotínin was a character in
Fonvízin's comedy *The Young Hopeful* – see the opening epigraph
and the note to p. 1. This expression comes in Act II, Sc. 3.

p. 98, *Mais laissez-moi donc, monsieur; mais êtes-vous fou?*:
"Let me alone, sir; are you mad?" (French).

A HISTORY OF GORYÚKHINO VILLAGE

p. 101, *on 1st April 1801*: All Fools' Day, 1st April, has been
celebrated across Europe, including Russia, for several centuries as a day for playing practical jokes. In 1825 Pushkin had
composed the following rhyme:

"In last night's north-easter,"
Tsar said with a frown –
"did you know? – Great Peter's
statue's been blown down!"
Courtier cried out, frightened,
"No! I'd no idea…"
Tsar's expression brightened:
"First of April's here!"

Clearly the date has been chosen by Pushkin here to indicate the satirical nature of this *History*. It is also probably inaccurate, as Belkin's friend's letter in the foreword to the *Stories* gives his year of birth more plausibly as 1798.

p. 101, *The Modern Primer*: A work by the savant, teacher and educationalist Nikolái Gavrílovich Kurgánov (1726–96), a professor at the Naval Academy and author of several books on mathematics, navigation and the Russian language. *The Modern Primer* was a popular and much reprinted work, first published in 1769 under the title *A Russian Universal Grammar, or General Primer Offering the Easiest Method of Basic Instruction in the Russian Language, with Seven Appendices Containing Various Instructive and Profitably Entertaining Material*. As well as a grammar it included sample letters, mythological and historical anecdotes, Russian proverbs, a selection of eighteenth-century Russian poetry and a miscellany of other information.

p. 101, *General Plemyánnikov*: Though not one of the most celebrated Russian generals, Pyótr Grigóryevich Plemyánnikov had a long and distinguished career in the Russian army, which he entered in 1725; a general from 1758, he played a leading role in the Russian-Turkish war of 1768–74; following the crucial Russian victory at Kagul in 1770 Catherine the Great rewarded him with the rank of general-in-chief; he retired in 1773 and died the same year. If Belkin Senior served as his adjutant, he must have been at least in his late forties by the time of his son's birth.

p. 102, *cloud of obscurity... empty myth*: Kurgánov's name, containing as it does the Russian word *kurgán* (tumulus, ancient burial mound), evokes a mythical, prehistoric past. The passage also suggests the gullible Belkin's inability to distinguish fiction and myth from true history.

p. 102, *Niebuhr*: Barthold Georg Niebuhr (1776–1831) was a Danish-German statesman, diplomat and historian; in his influential three-volume *Römische Geschichte* (1811–32) he subjected the legends of ancient Rome to critical scrutiny and reinterpretation and emphasized the importance of ethnographical evidence and genealogy. It was to Niebuhr, "the premier historian of our age", that the Russian writer Nikolái Alexéyevich Polevóy (1796–1846) had – pretentiously, in Pushkin's view – dedicated his six-volume *History of the Russian People* (1829–33), the first instalment of which Pushkin had reviewed harshly earlier in 1830 – see also the Extra Material on *A History of Goryúkhino Village* on p. 171.

p. 102, *Twelve Nations*: I.e. Napoleon's invading Grande Armée, which was said to be made up of soldiers from twelve nations.

p. 104, *much enduring Odysseus*: Homer describes in the *Odyssey* how the Greek hero Odysseus returns home from the ten-year Trojan war after ten more years of gruelling adventures. Though he is disguised, his old nurse Eurycleia recognizes him and, we are told, "delight and anguish swept through her heart together; her eyes were filled with tears; her voice was strangled by emotion" (*Odyssey* XIX, 471–72).

"Much enduring" (Greek πολύτλας) is one of Homer's standard epithets for Odysseus. Indeed, the whole sequence here – of unexpected arrival after a journey, warm bath, serving of food – is a skit on the treatment of heroic travellers in the *Odyssey* (see Telemachus's arrival at the palace of Menelaus and Helen in Book IV, and Odysseus's and his companions' visit to Circe's palace in Book X).

p. 105, *I finally received title… my patrimonial lands*: Pushkin himself, shortly after arriving at Bóldino, had been engaged in a similarly tedious bureaucratic process: Pushkin had been given ownership by his father, in anticipation of his marriage, of Kistenevo, an estate near Bóldino; Binyon (p. 340) explains: "On 11 September Pushkin sent a servant… with an application for the transfer of the serfs to the court at the district town, Sergach; and on the sixteenth… the district assessor… travelled to Kístenevo to induct Pushkin into his property. This did not, however, complete all the necessary formalities. The two hundred serfs had to be individually identified, and documents had to be prepared… [The servant] travelled backwards and forwards between Boldino and Sergach, and Pushkin himself, somewhat to his annoyance, had to ride twice… to the little town…"

p. 106, *Misanthropy and Remorse*: A sentimental drama (1789), very popular in its day, by the German writer August Friedrich Ferdinand von Kotzebue (1761–1819). Pushkin himself had attended a performance of the play with his fiancée in Moscow on 3rd May 1830. The role of Amalia ("Malchen"), a little girl of four, is a tiny one; she appears briefly at the very end of the play and says only two words; the part was usually played by a drama-school student.

p. 106, *the Well-Intentioned*: The *Well-Intentioned* (*Blagonamérenny* in Russian) was a literary journal published in St Petersburg between 1818 and 1826, of which Pushkin had a low opinion. It had a reputation for poor taste.

p. 106, *Hamburg Gazette*: Debreczeny comments as follows: "Pushkin probably means *Wöchentliche gemeinnützige Nachrichten von und für Hamburg* (later the *Hamburger Nachrichten*), which had been published since 1792 and was widely read in foreign countries as one of the most highly respected newspapers of the time."

p. 107, *That's B——, the writer*: In view here is the writer, journalist, reviewer and police agent Faddéi Venedíktovich Bulgárin (1789–1859), Pushkin's rival, critic and arch-enemy. Aitken and Budgen comment: "Bulgarin… was himself an incorrigible name-dropper. The passage contains numerous allusions to Bulgarin: most of the foreign items in his *Northern Bee* came straight from the *Hamburg Gazette*; several of his articles were published in [*The Champion of Enlightenment*]; and in 1824 he had written a 'Promenade along the Nevsky'; the meeting takes place at the 'Politseysky' Bridge, and the would-be writer is dressed in a 'pea-green' coat – a contemporary indication of a police inspector."

p. 107, *The Champion of Enlightenment*: A St Petersburg journal published between 1818 and 1826.

p. 107, *Politséysky Bridge*: The "Police Bridge" (also known as the Green Bridge) carrying the Nevsky Prospékt across the Moyka was so called because in the mid-eighteenth century the city's police headquarters and the police chief's residence were situated nearby. No doubt Pushkin is here hinting at his enemy Bulgárin's role as a police agent.

p. 108, *Ryúrik*: Ryúrik was a legendary Scandinavian adventurer of the ninth century, believed to have founded the Russian state and first ruling dynasty.

p. 108, *A Dangerous Neighbour*: A popular ribald and satirical poem written in 1811 by Pushkin's uncle Vasíly Lvovich Pushkin (1766–1830), the action of which is set in a brothel.

p. 108, *Critique of a Moscow Boulevard, To the Présnensky Ponds*: Anonymous satirical verses from the beginning of the nineteenth century, circulated in manuscript to avoid the attention of the censor.

p. 109, *the immortal achievement of Abbé Millot*: The French Jesuit teacher and historian Claude-François-Xavier Millot (1726–85) composed, among other historical works, a universal history entitled *Éléments d'histoire générale ancienne et moderne* (1772–83), published in Russia as *An Ancient and Modern History, from the Beginning of the World to the Present Time*.

p. 110, *Tatíshchev, Boltín and Gólikov*: Vasíly Nikítich Tatíshchev (1686–1750) wrote a *Russian History from Ancient Times* in five volumes, the first scholarly history of Russia, published after his death. Iván Nikítich Boltín (1735–92) and Iván Ivánovich Gólikov (1735–1801) were other early historians of Russia.

p. 110, *Old Slavonic numerals*: Old (Church) Slavonic, the language of the Russian Bible and of the Russian and other Slavonic Orthodox Churches, which was also employed for official documents and records in Muscovy before the eighteenth century, uses a cumbersome and archaic system of numerals represented by letters of the alphabet, inherited, through Byzantium, from ancient Greece. It is unsurprising that Belkin had difficulty with these numerals.

p. 111, *half a rouble in silver*: Compare this prize with the silver five-copeck piece with which "kind" Dunya rewarded the grateful little one-eyed ragamuffin at the end of 'The Postmaster' for conducting her to the cemetery.

p. 111, *unbroken series from 1744 to 1799… fifty-five years*: An example of Belkin's carelessness with facts – and ineptitude with figures. An unbroken series from 1744 to 1799 would cover fifty-six years. Under item 1 in the next section Belkin first gives the number of yearbooks as fifty-four, then splits them into two categories totalling fifty-five.

p. 112, *like a certain fellow historian… reflect on what I have achieved*: The historian whose name Belkin cannot remember is Edward Gibbon (1737–94), author of the celebrated *History of the Decline and Fall of the Roman Empire* (1776–88). In his *Memoirs of My Life and Writings* (1789, published posthumously), Gibbon, then living in Lausanne, describes his feelings after completing his great work. The passage reads as follows:

It was on the day, or rather night, of the 27th of June 1787, between the hours of eleven and twelve, that I wrote the last lines of the last page, in a summer house in my garden. After laying down my pen, I took several turns in a *berceau*, or covered walk of acacias, which commands a prospect of the country, the lake and the mountains. The air was temperate, the sky was serene, the silver orb of the moon was reflected from the waters, and all nature was silent. I will not dissemble the first emotions of joy on recovery of my freedom and, perhaps, the establishment of my fame. But my pride was soon humbled, and a sober melancholy was spread over my mind, by the idea that I had taken an everlasting leave of an old and agreeable companion, and that whatsoever might be the future fate of my History, the life of the historian must be short and precarious...

p. 112, *diacritical marks for abbreviations and figures*: These are the marks placed above letters in Church Slavonic script to indicate abbreviations or the use of letters as numerals (see second note to p. 110). The absence of these marks would make a document very hard to decipher.

p. 115, *of middling height... their hair is blond or ginger*: In his letter to the editor of *Belkin's Stories*, Belkin's neighbour describes him as of middling height, with grey eyes and fair hair, but his complexion, rather than "strong and vigorous" was "pale and gaunt", and Belkin testifies at the beginning of the *History* to his poor health.

p. 116, *Great-Russian*: "Great Russia" was the name used in tsarist times for the Russian-speaking heartland of the Empire, in contradistinction to "Little Russia", the name used for Ukraine.

p. 117, *various important events*: Very likely a reference to the Pugachóv Rebellion, a peasant uprising that raged across much of central Russia between 1773 and 1775.

p. 117, *He also plays… an important role in the history of Goryúkhino*: Terénty, however, is never mentioned again. Is this an example of Belkin's carelessness, or a casualty of Pushkin's failure to finish the *History*?

p. 117, *ancient public edifice… sign of the two-headed eagle*: Belkin is referring obliquely here to the village tavern. The state had a monopoly on the sale of liquor, and by a law of 1767 a representation of the two-headed eagle, emblem of the Russian Empire, had to be placed at the entrance to every tavern as a mark of its official status.

p. 117, *Eclogues of the renowned Virgil*: The pre-eminent Roman poet Virgil (Publius Vergilius Maro – 70–19 BC), most famous for his epic the *Aeneid*, also published a collection of ten short pastoral poems known as the *Eclogues*, set against a background of idealized rusticity.

p. 117, *idylls of Mr Sumarókov*: Alexándr Petróvich Sumarókov (1717–77) was a prolific dramatist and author of a wide variety of lyric poetry. Much influenced by the French classicism of the seventeenth and early eighteenth centuries, he was compared by enthusiastic Russian contemporaries to Boileau, Racine, Molière and La Fontaine. Later, however, his popularity waned. Pushkin had a low opinion of him.

p. 120, *The impoverished grandchildren... a tenth of what they had been*: This is a sentiment voiced by Pushkin before: in his unfinished *Novel in Letters* of 1829 he had had one of the correspondents write: "This is the reason for the rapid decline of our nobility: the grandfather was rich, the son lives in want, the grandson goes a-begging. Ancient families come to insignificance; new ones rise, but in the third generation disappear again."

p. 124, *The Regime of Estate Manager* —: In Pushkin's time landlords had almost unlimited power over the serfs on their estates. Absentee landlords (of whom there were many because they spent most of their time in the cities or owned multiple estates) would appoint estate managers with full responsibility for administering estates on their behalf, organizing payment of poll tax, selecting peasants for conscription in the army, etc.

Extra Material

on

Alexander Pushkin's

Belkin's Stories

and

*A History of
Goryúkhino Village*

Alexander Pushkin's Life

Alexander Pushkin (Alexándr Sergéyevich Pushkin) was born in Moscow in 1799. He came of an ancient, but largely undistin- guished aristocratic line. Some members of his father's family took part in the events of the reign of Tsar Borís Godunóv (1598–1605) and appear in Pushkin's historical drama about that Tsar. Perhaps his most famous ancestor – and the one of whom Pushkin was most proud – was his mother's grandfather, Abrám Petróvich Gannibál (or Annibál) (c.1693–1781), who was an African, most probably from Ethiopia or Cameroon. According to family tradition he was abducted from home at the age of seven by slave traders and taken to Istanbul. There in 1704 he was purchased by order of the Russian foreign minister and sent to Moscow, where the minister made a gift of him to Tsar Peter the Great. Peter took a liking to the boy and in 1707 stood godfather to him at his christening (hence his patronymic Petróvich, "son of Peter"). Later Abrám adopted the surname "Gannibál", a Russian transliteration of Hannibal, the famous African general of Roman times. Peter sent him abroad as a young man to study fortification and military mining. After seven years in France he was recalled to Russia, where he followed a career as a military engineer. Peter's daughter, the Empress Elizabeth, made him a general, and he eventually died in retirement well into his eighties on one of the estates granted him by the crown.

Pushkin had an older sister, Olga, and a younger brother, Lev. His parents did not show him much affection as a child, and he was left to the care of his grandmother and servants, including a nurse of whom he became very fond. As was usual in those days, his early schooling was received at home, mostly from French tutors and in the French language.

School　　In 1811, at the age of twelve, Pushkin was sent by his parents to St Petersburg to be educated at the new Lyceum (Lycée, or high school) that the Emperor Alexander I had just established in a wing of his summer palace at Tsárskoye Seló to prepare the sons of noblemen for careers in the government service. Pushkin spent six happy years there, studying (his curriculum included Russian, French, Latin, German, state economy and finance, scripture, logic, moral philosophy, law, history, geography, statistics and mathematics), socializing with teachers and fellow students and relaxing in the palace park. To the end of his life he remained deeply attached to his memories and friends from those years. In 1817 he graduated with the rank of collegial secretary, the tenth rank in the civil service, and was attached to the Ministry of Foreign Affairs, with duties that he was allowed to interpret as minimal. While still at the Lyceum, Pushkin had already started writing poetry, some of which had attracted the admiration of leading Russian literary figures of the time.

St Petersburg　Pushkin spent the next three years in St Petersburg living a life
1817–20　　of pleasure and dissipation. He loved the company of friends, drinking parties, cards, the theatre and particularly women. He took an interest in radical politics. And he continued to write poetry – mostly lyric verses and epigrams on personal, amatory or political subjects – often light and ribald, but always crisply, lucidly and elegantly expressed. Some of these verses, even unpublished, gained wide currency in St Petersburg and attracted the unfavourable notice of the Emperor.

Pushkin's major work of this period was *Ruslan and Lyudmila*, a mock epic in six cantos, published in 1820 and enthusiastically received by the public. Before it could be published, however, the Emperor finally lost patience with the subversiveness of some of Pushkin's shorter verses and determined to remove him from the capital. He first considered exiling Pushkin to Siberia or the White Sea; but at the intercession of high-placed friends of Pushkin's the proposed sentence was commuted to a posting to the south of Russia. Even so, some supposed friends hurt and infuriated Pushkin by spreading exaggerated rumours about his disgrace.

Pushkin was detailed to report to Lieutenant General Iván Inzóv (1768–1845), who was at the time Chairman of the Board of Trustees for the Interests of Foreign Colonists in Southern Russia based at Yekaterinosláv (now Dnepropetróvsk) on the lower Dnieper. Inzóv gave him a friendly welcome, but little work to do, and before long Pushkin caught a fever from bathing in the river and was confined to bed in his poor lodgings. He was rescued by General Nikolái Rayévsky, a soldier who had distinguished himself in the war of 1812 against Napoleon. Rayévsky, who from 1817 to 1824 commanded the Fourth Infantry Corps in Kiev, was travelling through Yekaterinosláv with his younger son (also called Nikolái), his two youngest daughters María and Sófya, a personal physician and other attendants; they were on their way to join the elder son Alexander, who was taking a cure at the mineral springs in the Caucasus. General Rayévsky generously invited Pushkin to join them; and Inzóv gave his leave.

The party arrived in Pyatigórsk, in the northern foothills of the Caucasus, in June. Pushkin, along with his hosts, benefited from the waters and was soon well again. He accompanied the Rayévskys on long trips into the surrounding country, where he enjoyed the mountain scenery and observed the way of life of the local Circassian and Chechen tribes. In early August they set off westwards to join the rest of the Rayévsky family (the General's wife and two older daughters) in the Crimea. On the way they passed through the Cossack-patrolled lands on the northern bank of the Kubán river and learnt more about the warlike Circassians of the mountains to the south.

General Rayévsky and his party including Pushkin met up with the rest of the family at Gurzúf on the Crimean coast, where they had the use of a villa near the shore. Pushkin enjoyed his time in the Crimea, particularly the majestic coastal scenery, the southern climate and the new experience of living in the midst of a harmonious, hospitable and intelligent family. He also fell in love with Yekaterína, the General's eldest daughter, a love that was not reciprocated. Before leaving the Crimea, Pushkin travelled with the Rayévskys through the coastal mountains and inland to Bakhchisaráy, an oriental town which had till forty years before been the capital of the Tatar khans of the Crimea and where the khans' palace still stood (and stands).

After a month in the Crimea it was time for the party to return to the mainland. During the summer General Inzóv had been transferred from Yekaterinosláv to be governor of Bessarabia (the northern slice of Moldavia, which Russia had annexed from Turkey only eight years previously). His new headquarters was in Kishinyóv (today, Chişinău), the chief town of Bessarabia. So it was to Kishinyóv that Pushkin went back to duty in September 1820. Pushkin remained there (with spells of local leave) till 1823.

Bessarabia
1820–23
Kishinyóv was still, apart from recently arrived Russian officials and soldiers, a raw Near Eastern town, with few buildings of stone or brick, populated by Moldavians and other Balkan nationalities. Despite the contrast with St Petersburg, Pushkin still passed a lot of his time in a similar lifestyle of camaraderie, drinking, gambling, womanizing and quarrelling, with little official work. But he wrote too. And he also, as in the Caucasus and Crimea, took a close interest in the indigenous cultures, visiting local fairs and living for a few days with a band of Moldavian gypsies, an experience on which he later drew in his narrative poem *Gypsies*.

In the winter of 1820–21 Pushkin finished the first of his "southern" narrative poems, *A Prisoner in the Caucasus*, which he had already begun in the Crimea. (The epilogue he added in May 1821.) This poem reflects the experiences of his Caucasus visit. The work was published in August 1822. It had considerable public success, not so much for the plot and characterization, which were criticized even by Pushkin himself; but rather, as the author acknowledged, for its "truthful, though only lightly sketched descriptions of the Caucasus and the customs of its mountain peoples".

Having completed *A Prisoner in the Caucasus*, Pushkin went on to write a narrative poem reflecting his impressions of the Crimea, *The Fountain of Bakhchisaray*. This was started in 1821, finished in 1823, and published in March 1824. It was also a great popular success, though again Pushkin dismissed it as "rubbish". Both poems, as Pushkin admitted, show the influence of Lord Byron, a poet whom, particularly at this period, Pushkin admired.

Just before his departure from Kishinyóv in 1823, Pushkin composed the first few stanzas of Chapter I of his greatest work, the novel-in-verse *Eugene Onegin*. It took him eight years to complete. Each chapter was published separately (except Chapters IV and V, which came out together) between the years 1825 and 1832; the work was first published as a whole in 1833.

In the summer of 1823, through the influence of his friends in St Petersburg, Pushkin was posted to work for Count Mikhaíl Vorontsóv, who had just been appointed Governor General of the newly Russianized region south of the Ukraine. Vorontsóv's headquarters were to be in Odessa, the port city on the Black Sea founded by Catherine the Great thirty years previously. Despite its newness Odessa was a far more lively, cosmopolitan and cultured place than Kishinyóv, and Pushkin was pleased with the change. But he only remained there a year. *Odessa 1823–24*

Pushkin did not get on well with his new chief, partly because of temperamental differences, partly because Pushkin objected to the work Count Vorontsóv expected him to do, and partly because Pushkin had an affair with the Countess. Vorontsóv tried hard to get Pushkin transferred elsewhere, and Pushkin for his part became so unhappy with his position on the Count's staff that he tried to resign and even contemplated escaping overseas. But before matters came to a head the police intercepted a letter from Pushkin to a friend in which he spoke approvingly of the atheistic views of an Englishman he had met in the city. The authorities in St Petersburg now finally lost patience with Pushkin: he was dismissed from the service and sent to indefinite banishment on his mother's country estate of Mikháylovskoye in the west of Russia. He left Odessa for Mikháylovskoye on 1st August 1824; he had by now written two and a half chapters of *Eugene Onegin*, and had begun *Gypsies*.

Pushkin spent more than two years under police surveillance at Mikháylovskoye. The enforced leisure gave him a lot of time for writing. Within a couple of months he had completed *Gypsies*, which was first published in full in 1827. *Gypsies* is a terser, starker, more thoughtful and dramatic *Exile at Mikháylovskoye* work than *A Prisoner in the Caucasus* or *The Fountain of Bakhchisaray*; along with *Eugene Onegin* it marks a transition from the discursive romanticism of Pushkin's earliest years to the compressed realism of his mature style. At Mikháylovskoye Pushkin completed Chapters III–VI of *Eugene Onegin*, many passages of which reflect Pushkin's observation of country life and love of the countryside. He also wrote his historical drama *Boris Godunov* at this period and his entertaining verse tale *Count Nulin*.

The Decembrist Revolt 1825

In November 1825 Alexander I died. He had no legitimate children, and there was initially confusion over the succession. In December some liberally minded members of the army and the intelligentsia (subsequently known as the "Decembrists") seized the opportunity to attempt a *coup d'état*. This was put down by the new Emperor Nicholas I, a younger brother of Alexander's. Among the conspirators were several old friends of Pushkin's; and he might well have joined them had he been at liberty. As it was, the leading conspirators were executed, and many of the rest were sent to Siberia for long spells of hard labour and exile. Pushkin feared that he too might be punished.

Rehabilitation 1826–31

The following autumn Pushkin was summoned unexpectedly to Moscow to see the new Emperor. Nicholas surprised Pushkin by offering him his freedom, and Pushkin assured Nicholas of his future good conduct. Pushkin complained that he had difficulty in making money from his writing because of the censorship, and Nicholas undertook to oversee Pushkin's work personally. In practice, however, the Emperor delegated the task to the Chief of the Secret Police and, despite occasional interventions from Nicholas, Pushkin continued to have difficulty with the censors.

After a few months in Moscow Pushkin returned to St Petersburg, where he spent most of his time in the coming years, though he continued periodically to visit Moscow, call at the family's estates and stay with friends in the country. In 1829 he made his only visit abroad: after revisiting the Caucasus he followed the Russian army on a campaign into north-eastern Turkey. During the late 1820s he made several attempts to find a wife, with a view to settling down. In 1829 he met Natálya

Goncharóva: they were engaged in 1830 and married early in 1831.

It was during the four years between his return from exile and his marriage that he wrote Chapter VII (1827–28) and most of Chapter VIII (1829–31) of *Eugene Onegin*. In 1828 he also wrote *Poltava* (published in 1829), a kind of novella-in-verse based on the study of historical material. In its application of the imagination to real historical events, it prefigured Pushkin's later historical novel in prose, *The Captain's Daughter*, and helped to set a pattern for subsequent historical novels in Russia. It is also notable for the terse realism of its descriptions and for the pace and drama of its narratives and dialogues. It was during this period, too, that Pushkin began to write fiction in prose, though it was not till late in 1830 that he succeeded in bringing any prose stories to completion.

In the autumn of 1830 a cholera epidemic caused Pushkin to be marooned for a couple of months on another family estate, Bóldino, some 600 kilometres east of Moscow. He took advantage of the enforced leisure to write. It was at this time that he composed *Belkin's Stories* and *A History of Goryúkhino Village*. He also completed Chapter VIII of *Onegin*, another verse tale called *The Little House in Kolomna*, many lyrics and his set of four one-act dramas known together as *The Little Tragedies*.

The 1830s were not on the whole happy years for Pushkin. His marriage, it is true, was more successful than might have been expected. Natálya was thirteen years his junior; her remarkable beauty and susceptibility to admiration constantly exposed her to the attentions of other men; she showed more liking for society and its entertainments than for intellectual or artistic pursuits or for household management; her fashionable tastes and social aspirations incurred outlays that the pair could ill afford; and she took little interest in her husband's writing. Nonetheless, despite all this they seem to have remained a loyal and loving couple; Natálya bore him four children in their less than six years of marriage, and she showed real anguish at his untimely death.

But there were other difficulties. Pushkin, though short of money himself and with a costly family of his own to maintain,

The Final Years
1831–37

was often called upon to help out his parents, his brother and sister and his in-laws, and so fell ever deeper into debt. Both his wife and the Emperor demanded his presence in the capital so that he would be available to attend social and court functions, while he would much have preferred to be in the country, writing. Though Nicholas gave him intermittent support socially and financially, many at court and in the government, wounded by his jibes or shocked by his supposed political and sexual liberalism, disliked or despised him. And a new generation of writers and readers were beginning to look on him as a man of the past.

In 1831 Pushkin at length completed *Eugene Onegin*. The eighth and final chapter was published at the beginning of 1832, the first complete edition of the work coming out in 1833. But overall in these years Pushkin wrote less; and when he did write he turned increasingly to prose. In 1833 he spent another productive autumn at the Bóldino estate, producing his most famous prose novella *The Queen of Spades* and one of the finest of his narrative poems *The Bronze Horseman*. He also developed in these years his interest in history, already evident in *Boris Godunov* and *Poltava*: Nicholas I commissioned him to write a history of Peter the Great, but alas he only left copious notes for this at his death. He did, however, write in 1833 his *History of Pugachov*, a well-researched account of the eighteenth-century Cossack and peasant uprising under Yemelyán Pugachóv, which Nicholas allowed him to publish in 1834. He built on his research into this episode to write his longest work of prose fiction, the historical novel *The Captain's Daughter* (1836). Over these years too he produced his five verse fairy stories; these are mostly based on Russian folk tales, but one, *The Golden Cockerel* (1834), is an adaptation of one of Washington Irving's *Tales of the Alhambra*.

Writings   From his schooldays till his death Pushkin also composed well over 600 shorter poems, including many lyrics of love and friendship, brief narratives, protests, invectives, epigrams, epitaphs and dedications. He left numerous letters from his adult years that give us an invaluable insight into his thoughts and activities and those of his contemporaries. And as a man of keen intelligence and interest in literature, he produced throughout his career many articles and shorter notes – some published in his lifetime, others not – containing a wide variety of literary criticism and comment.

Early in 1837 Pushkin's career was cut tragically short. *Death* Following a series of improper advances to his wife and insults to himself, he felt obliged to fight a duel with a young Frenchman who was serving as an officer in the imperial horse guards in St Petersburg. Pushkin was fatally wounded in the stomach and died at his home in St Petersburg two days later. The authorities denied him a public funeral in the capital for fear of demonstrations, and he was buried privately at the Svyatýe Gory monastery near Mikháylovskoye, where his memorial has remained a place of popular pilgrimage.

Belkin's Stories

On the surface *Belkin's Stories* is a straightforward work: five fast-moving, often humorous, sometimes moving narratives, prefaced by a short foreword. But there are underlying complexities.

The first complexity is in the foreword itself. We are told that an editor, "A.P.", has come into possession of five stories, compiled by an Iván Petróvich Belkin, now deceased. "A.P." makes enquiries about Belkin, whom he never knew, and receives information in a letter from a friend of the dead man. The foreword consists of little more than a transcript of this letter. It transpires that Belkin, an obscure country landowner, was not the creator of the stories, but had heard them from others, who in three cases ('The Shot', 'The Blizzard' and 'The Postmaster') depended on yet others for important sections of the narrative.

But Pushkin is having us on. Though the stories are said to be "in large part true", they are actually fictions related by fictional storytellers to a fictional compiler (about whom we are informed by a fictional friend) and published by the enigmatic editor "A.P.", who may or may not be the real-life Alexander Pushkin (readers of the first, anonymous edition were left in doubt).

Why did Pushkin create this complex fantasy as a frame for the stories? Seemingly for several reasons. First, Pushkin liked blurring the boundaries between reality and fiction, to make the

reader believe an imagined story to be true. Here he presents
the five stories within a framework of circumstances, the very
complexity and banality of which enhances the stories' plausi-
bility. Secondly, Pushkin is striving to distance the true author
(himself) from the stories: paradoxically, the very remoteness of
the stories from any real-life author, at the far end of a fictitious
chain of transmission, projects an illusion of their objectivity
and reality. Thirdly, Pushkin used Belkin as a way of bringing
unity to a group of otherwise disparate narratives. And fourthly,
Pushkin loved a jest, and uses the elaborate frame within which
the stories are presented to tease his readers.

Another complexity of *Belkin's Stories* consists in the literary parody pervading them. This aspect of Pushkin's writing is
hard for us to appreciate now, less familiar as we are with the
objects of his parody – the Greek and Roman classics, the Bible
and French, Russian and other literatures of the early nineteenth
and preceding centuries, in all of which Pushkin was extremely
well read. For Pushkin and his contemporaries "parody" did
not necessarily imply mockery; it could mean simply the quotation and imitation of other authors, often with admiration
and goodwill, in order to develop one's literary style, flatter the
literary awareness of readers or entertain them by subverting
their expectations.

Pushkin also used parody as a motor for plot: in each of the
five stories Pushkin has one of the main personalities attempt
to act out the part of a character from popular fiction – in
'The Shot' it is the swashbuckling fighter and jealous love
rival; in 'The Blizzard' the besotted lover; in 'The Undertaker'
the casual dabbler in the occult; in 'The Postmaster' the father
abandoned by his child; and in 'Young Miss Peasant' the aristocratic philanderer – and Pushkin shows in each case how real
life can frustrate such attempted role play with unpredictable
consequences, benign or tragic.

The clearest and most sustained example of Pushkin's use of
parody, in the sense just described, is in 'The Postmaster', where
Pushkin makes extensive use of Chapter 15 of St Luke's Gospel
in the New Testament. The chapter contains three of Christ's
parables, the chief of which is the parable of the prodigal son

(vv. 11–32), which is summarized in the four prints the narrator observes on the postmaster's wall. It is these prints that subliminally condition the expectations of the postmaster, the narrator and the reader. As the story unfolds it becomes clear that the postmaster, only too familiar with the illustrations on his wall, casts himself in the role of the abandoned father; Dunya he imagines as a "prodigal daughter" indulging in "dissolute behaviour" in the city and subsequently reduced to penury, rags and starvation. He longs to welcome her back home like the old father in the fourth print. The father's tragedy is to misapply the parable, intended to illustrate God's relation to humanity, to his own relationship with his daughter: in other words, unconsciously he is putting himself in the role of God as creator and master of his human offspring, and treats Dunya, despite his affection for her, as his property, to serve him as domestic drudge, not as a fellow human being with a right, as she reaches maturity, to make a life for herself. Tragically it is the postmaster who eventually dies in alcoholic degradation and despair – almost a prodigal father – before his daughter comes back to reveal that the life she has found for herself is evidently a happy, prosperous and fulfilling one.

Earlier in Luke 15 there are two other similar parables. The first is the parable of the lost sheep (vv. 3–7): the caring shepherd goes in search of the lost sheep to bring it back home. But once more the postmaster misapplies the parable and imagines himself, God-like, going off to St Petersburg to "bring home my little lost sheep".

In the third parable (Luke 15:8–10), Christ makes his point again by telling of a woman with ten silver coins who loses one and searches her house till she recovers it. At the close of 'The Postmaster' a silver coin is mentioned three times, but not to be recovered and hoarded. Both Dunya and the narrator make a gift of a silver five-copeck coin to the grateful little one-eyed ragamuffin. Rather than hoarding something precious as the postmaster attempted, Pushkin seems to be asking, is it not better to give it away?

A third layer of complexity in the stories is autobiography: as elsewhere in his works, Pushkin includes covert references to his own life. In particular, all these stories revolve around marriage or death or both, reflecting Pushkin's own situation in 1830. While writing the *Stories* Pushkin was engaged to be married. So, as leading characters in four of the stories – the Count, Burmín, Dunya and Alexéi – move from a flirtatious and devil-may-care youth towards a more level-headed and staid maturity in wedlock, Pushkin is seeing himself about to undergo the same transformation. Pushkin was also at the time marooned in remote Bóldino, surrounded by death and fear of death from a national cholera epidemic. So both marriage and death were much in Pushkin's mind at the time.

The most extensive use of autobiographical reference comes in 'The Undertaker', where features of the undertaker's life and character reflect Pushkin's view of himself at the time. Adrián Prókhorov's initials A.P. are also Pushkin's. The year 1799, when Prókhorov sold his first coffin, was the year of Pushkin's birth (in Moscow). Pushkin seems to have seen parallels between the trades of undertaker and poet in the loneliness and professional isolation they both imposed and in the low esteem in which they were held. Prókhorov worked at his trade on Basmánnaya "in a tumbledown shack" for eighteen years before moving to more salubrious quarters on Nikítskaya, which he had long desired but where, on his arrival, he felt "no joy in his heart". Pushkin, after eighteen years as a footloose bachelor and writer (he wrote his first poem in 1813), was now, in the autumn of 1830, expecting within months to marry a fiancée who lived in a large mansion on Nikítskaya. Pushkin had long wanted to marry, but as marriage drew near he often felt dread at the prospect, sometimes envisaging his prospective marriage as the death of the old Pushkin. Prókhorov's new signboard of a "plump cupid with a downturned torch in his hand" seems to symbolize Pushkin's realization that the free love life he had enjoyed for so long would have to end with his change of status; and the coffins and "ageing stock" of funeral paraphernalia cluttering the kitchen and living room stand for Pushkin's past literary output, now less popular than it had been. On one level, therefore, the story can be read as a sardonic parable of Pushkin's apprehensive feelings on moving away from his familiar bachelor life to the costlier situation of marriage, which might end in nightmare – or might not. Thus the central story of the five, the only one not dealing explicitly with marriage, also turns out to deal with it in a veiled manner.

A political subtext is also traceable in places. Overt social and political criticism was precluded by rigid censorship under Nicholas I's regime. Nonetheless, many characters and storylines throughout the *Stories* reflect Pushkin's sympathy with the small man or woman and his impatience with Russia's hierarchical and unjust social system and its demeaning consequences for individuals and society.

The foreword, however, seems to contain a more sensitive, though carefully coded, political reference. Belkin's friend is confused over dates: he opens his letter by stating that he received A.P.'s letter of the 15th [November 1830] on the 23rd of the month, but ends by dating his reply 16th November. He also claims to have forgotten the number of the light-infantry regiment in which Belkin enlisted in 1815 and omits, surprisingly, to mention Belkin's rank on retiring from the army in 1823. There are grounds for regarding these errors and omissions as deliberate. The friend's confusion over Belkin's military career and over the dating of the correspondence highlights the figures 15, 23 and 16: (18)15 was the year in which Belkin enlisted in the army, (18)23 was the year in which he was discharged, and part of the 16th infantry division had been based in Kishinyóv at the time when Pushkin was stationed there in the early 1820s; the officers – many, his friends – were notorious for their liberal views, and during 1822 and 1823 the anxious government had a number of them removed. Is Pushkin hinting that it was the 16th infantry division in which Belkin had enlisted and that he was one of those whose overly liberal views led to their discharge in 1822–23, without the expected promotion and even in disgrace? That supposition would tally with Belkin's introduction of markedly liberal reforms in the treatment of his peasants when he returned home and might explain his more cautious and conservative neighbour's diplomatic reluctance to identify Belkin's regiment and to have himself named as a friend of such a politically suspect character. It may be that Pushkin is sketching, in Belkin, an affectionate, if satirical portrait, indecipherable by the censor, of a liberal-minded junior army officer such as those with whom he socialized during his stay in Kishinyóv – idealistic if ineffectual men, many of whom went on to participate in the botched Decembrist revolt of 1825. The foreword thus can be read as a coded memorial to the executed or exiled activists of the movement and to their demoralized and disillusioned sympathizers.

Pushkin's contemporaries were mostly deceived and disappointed by the work's apparent artlessness. But later generations have come to appreciate its humour, its vitality, its insights and its compassion, along with its other subtleties.

A History of Goryúkhino Village

Though related to *Belkin's Stories* through its supposed author, Iván Petróvich Belkin, and his home village Goryúkhino, the *History* is a separate work. Pushkin dated the manuscript 31st October and 1st November, so it seems that he commenced the *History* at Bóldino in late October 1830, soon after finishing the *Stories*. Pushkin never completed or published the *History*. It first appeared, in censored form, after his death in 1837.

Pushkin was deeply interested in history; and before his death he was to publish serious works of pure history (*A History of Pugachóv*) and historical fiction (*The Captain's Daughter*). It is curious, therefore, that his first sustained essay in the genre should be neither serious nor historical: *A History of Goryúkhino Village* is comedy, a spoof history of a fictitious rural community.

One element of the comedy is the personality of the supposed author. The foreword to *Belkin's Stories* had presented Belkin as an ineffectual, if liberal-minded young landowner. Here the portrait is filled out in the lengthy autobiographical introduction and in the later paragraphs of supposed history, revealing the would-be historian as someone peculiarly unsuited to the writing of history. On his own admission Belkin's education has been deficient; his memory is poor; his health is frail; he has difficulty with numbers; his intellect is weak; he cannot distinguish the important from the trivial, is easily sidetracked into irrelevancies, and is incapable of applying discipline or logic to the arrangement of his material; his narrative is careless and inaccurate; he is gullible and lacks awareness of human nature; he has little energy or initiative. Some historian! But there are also more serious strata in the work.

Pushkin used the *History* for a parodic critique of portentous historiography in general. One target was clearly Nikolái Polevóy, who had recently published two volumes of his own *History of the Russian People*. Pushkin had criticized Polevóy for his adulation of Niebuhr and for his incoherent ethnographical account of Russia's origins; and had commented on the errors and contradictions resulting from the reckless haste in which Polevóy had written. Belkin's historical approach reflects these criticisms.

At a deeper level is a satirical critique of the rural society and economy of contemporary Russia – landlords incompetent and ineffective or grasping and cruel, peasants ignorant or boorish, downtrodden and stultified by serfdom. It was doubtless the political sensitivity of this element, veiled though it was, that discouraged Pushkin from finishing the work and submitting it to an unsympathetic censor.

There is also self-parody in Pushkin's portrayal of Belkin. Like Pushkin, Belkin belongs to an ancient noble family, whose estates are diminished by multiple inheritance and poor management. And Pushkin parodies his own literary career in describing Belkin, like himself, as attempting to write poetry before "lowering himself to prose writing". Pushkin makes fun, too, of his own predilection for "clarity and concision" as the marks of good prose style when he has Belkin praise these qualities in his great-grandfather's terse diary entries.

A History of Goryúkhino Village, even in its unfinished state, is a work of pervasive humour and penetrating observation on several levels.

– Roger Clarke
April 2014

Translator's Note

My main aim as translator has been simple: to reproduce in contemporary English the "clarity and concision" that Pushkin made the hallmarks of his prose. Though Pushkin maintained these qualities through most of the *Stories* and the *History*, he did make occasional departures (in A.P.'s editorial foreword for example) for purposes of characterization or parody, and there I have tried to modulate the translation accordingly.

In transliterating Russian names I have used the British Standard method in its simplified version. This still leaves the reader without guidance on stress, which is both important and unpredictable in Russian. I have, therefore, normally marked the stressed syllable of Russian names with an acute accent on the appropriate vowel, except where these are monosyllables or words of two syllables with the stress on the first (e.g. "Pushkin", "Belkin").

Most Russian surnames have a distinct feminine form, and in accordance with usual practice I have used these for women.

Except when on familiar terms, Russians usually refer to each other by forename and patronymic (that is, the forename of the father suffixed with "-ovich" or "-evich" for men and "-ovna" or "-evna" for women). For the sake of authenticity I have retained this usage in my translation.

All dates are given in Old Style.

Select Bibliography

RUSSIAN TEXTS OF BELKIN'S STORIES AND A HISTORY OF GORYÚKHINO VILLAGE

Sobrániye Sochinéniy Púshkina (Moscow: Gosudárstvennoye Izdátelstvo Khudózhestvennoy Literatúry, 1959–62) Vol. v. This ten-volume collection of Pushkin's works is also available online through the *Rússkaya virtuálnaya bibliotéka* at www.rvb.ru/pushkin/toc.htm.

Pólnoye Sobrániye Sochinéniy Púshkina v Dvukh Tomákh, Vol. II (Moscow: Izdátelsky Tsentr Klássika, 1999)

Pushkin, A.S., *Tales of the Late Iván Petróvich Belkin*, edited with introduction and bibliography by A.D.P. Briggs, notes and glossary by B.O. Unbegaun (Bristol: Bristol Classical Press, 1994)

ENGLISH EDITIONS

Pushkin, A.S., *Complete Works of Alexander Pushkin*, Vol. VIII, translated (with notes) by Gillon Aitken and David Budgen (London: Angel Books, 1982)

Pushkin, A.S., *Complete Prose Fiction*, translated, with an introduction and notes, by Paul Debreczeny (Stanford, CA: Stanford University Press, 1983)

BOOKS AND ARTICLES ABOUT BELKIN'S STORIES
AND A HISTORY OF GORYÚKHINO VILLAGE

van der Eng, Jan M.; van Holk, A.G.F.; Meijer, Jan M., *The Tales of Belkin by A.S. Puškin* (The Hague: Mouton & Co N.V., 1968)

Gregg, Richard, 'A Scapegoat for all Seasons: the Unity and Shape of *The Tales of Belkin*', in *Slavic Review* 30, no. 4 (1971), pp. 748–61

Shaw, J.T., 'Pushkin's *The Stationmaster* and the New Testament Parable' in *Slavic and Eastern European Journal* Vol. 21, No. 1 (1977), pp. 3–29 (American Association of Teachers of Slavic and East European Languages)

Kodjak, Andrej, *Pushkin's I.P. Belkin* (Columbus, OH: Slavica Publishers, 1979)

Bethea, David M. and Davydov, Sergei, 'Pushkin's Saturnine Cupid: The Poetics of Parody in *The Tales of Belkin*', in *PMLA* Vol. 96, No. 1 (1981), pp. 8–21 (Modern Language Association of America)

Bethea, David M. and Davydov, Sergei, '*The [Hi]story of the Village of Gorjuxino*: In Praise of Pushkin's Folly', in *The Slavic and East European Journal*, Vol. 28, No. 3 (Autumn

1984), pp. 291–309 (American Association of Teachers of Slavic and East European Languages)

BIOGRAPHIES OF PUSHKIN

Lotman, Yury Mikháylovich, *Alexándr Sergéyevich Pushkin: biográfiya pisátelya* (St Petersburg: Iskússtvo-SPB, 1995)
Binyon, T.J.: *Pushkin: A Biography* (London: HarperCollins, 2002)

OTHER BOOKS ABOUT PUSHKIN AND HIS WORK

Tomashévsky, B.: *Pushkin*, (Moscow-Leningrad: Izdátelstvo Akadémii Naúk SSSR, 1956)
Bayley, John, *Pushkin: A Comparative Commentary* (Cambridge, Cambridge University Press, 1971)
Briggs, A.D.P., *Alexander Pushkin: A Critical Study* (London: Croom Helm, 1983)
Wolff, Tatiana, ed., *Pushkin on Literature* (London: Athlone Press, 1986)

Acknowledgements

My thanks go to two people especially – to Alessandro Gallenzi of Alma Classics for entrusting me with the happy task of translating and editing these fascinating and entertaining works of Pushkin's; and to Elizabeth, my wife, for her unfailing support and help throughout my work.

I am grateful too to Simon Blundell, librarian of the Reform Club in London, who provided me with prompt and invaluable help in my research; and to Christian Müller and the rest of the editorial team at Alma Classics, for their efficiency and patience in processing the text and in accommodating my requests. Remaining faults are my own.

– Roger Clarke

April 2014